Collins

SNAP REVISION

NEVER LET ME GO

AQA GCSE English Literature

D0293137

KRISTA CARSON

REVISE SET TEXTS IN A SNAP

Published by Collins
An imprint of HarperCollinsPublishers
1 London Bridge Street,
London, SE1 9GF

9780008247140

First published 2017

10 9 8 7 6 5 4 3 2 1

British Library Cataloguing in Publication Data.

A CIP record of this book is available from the
British Library.

Printed in the UK by Martins the Printer Ltd.

Commissioning Editor: Gillian Bowman
Managing Editor: Craig Balfour
Author: Krista Carson
Copyeditor: David Christie
Proofreaders: Jill Laidlaw and Louise Robb
Project management and typesetting:
  Mark Steward
Cover designers: Kneath Associates and
  Sarah Duxbury
Production: Natalia Rebow

ACKNOWLEDGEMENTS

Quotations from *Never Let Me Go* by Kazuo
Ishiguro © *Never Let Me Go*, Kazuo Ishiguro,
Faber and Faber Ltd

The author and publisher are grateful to the
copyright holders for permission to use quoted
materials and images.

Every effort has been made to trace copyright
holders and obtain their permission for the use of
copyright material. The author and publisher will
gladly receive information enabling them to rectify
any error or omission in subsequent editions. All
facts are correct at time of going to press.

Contents

You must be able to: understand what happens in the second half of Part Two.

What happens?

In Chapter 14, the group go to where Rodney first saw Ruth's possible; from a distance, they all agree that she bears a resemblance to Ruth. However, when they later follow the woman into an art gallery, they realise, upon closer inspection, that she is nothing like Ruth.

Ruth becomes angry, stating that it was never going to be her possible because they are **modelled** on trash – unwanted people in society – not fully functional members of society.

Ruth, Chrissie and Rodney go to visit Martin, a former veteran from the Cottages who is now a carer.

In Chapter 15, Kathy and Tommy refuse to visit Martin, so they spend the afternoon searching for Kathy's lost Judy Bridgewater tape in second-hand stores. Eventually, they find it and Tommy buys it for Kathy.

Tommy tells Kathy that artwork is important to their future and that he has been creating art recently. He describes how Miss Emily once said that it revealed their souls. He proposes a theory, where the artwork collected by Madame is used to help former students get deferrals because it can be used to prove that they are truly in love.

When Ruth finds out about the tape in Chapter 16, she initially doesn't react. However, Ruth is hurt when she finds out that Tommy told Kathy about his theory before telling her. She criticises Tommy's artwork and suggests that Kathy also finds it humorous.

In Chapter 17, Kathy confronts Ruth about Tommy's unhappiness. Ruth admits that they may not stay together forever. However, she tells Kathy that Tommy does not have romantic feelings for her.

Soon after, Kathy applies to begin her training.

How is Ruth presented in this section of the text?

Ruth is eager to please the older veterans. She ignores Tommy and Kathy when the veterans are around, often putting them down in order to gain acceptance.

She also fabricates stories about Hailsham, which puts her in a position of power over others, especially veterans such as Chrissie and Rodney.

Ruth has dreams of working in an office, even though everyone knows this will never happen. This is what makes finding her possible in an office so enticing for her.

Her relationship with Tommy is rocky throughout this section of the text. She appears jealous of the relationship Tommy has with Kathy, which is why she tells Kathy that, even if they do break up, Tommy will never like her in that way.

Key Quotations to Learn

'We're modelled from *trash*. Junkies, prostitutes, winos, tramps. Convicts, maybe, just so long as they're not psychos.' (Ruth: Chapter 14)

'Suppose two people come up and say they're in love. She can find the art they've done over years and years. She can see if they go. If they match.' (Tommy: Chapter 15)

'Well, Kathy, what you have to realise is that Tommy doesn't see you like that. He really, really likes you, he thinks you're really great. But I know he doesn't see you like, you know, a proper girlfriend.' (Ruth: Chapter 17)

Summary

- The group are disappointed when the possible turns out to look nothing like Ruth.
- Tommy discusses his theory that their artwork can help prove they are in love.
- Ruth tells Kathy that Tommy does not care about her in a romantic way.

Questions

QUICK TEST
1. How does Ruth react to discovering that the woman is not her possible?
2. What do Tommy and Kathy find while in Cromer?
3. What is Tommy's theory about Madame's Gallery?
4. What does Ruth tell Kathy about Tommy?

EXAM PRACTICE
Using one or more of the 'Key Quotations to Learn', write about the character of Ruth.

Part Three (Chapters 18 to 20)

You must be able to: understand what happens in the first half of Part Three.

What happens?

At the start of Chapter 18, Kathy says that seven or more years have passed since she left the Cottages. She runs into an old friend, Laura, who tells her that Ruth has had a bad first donation. Laura suggests that Kathy become Ruth's carer. They also discuss the closure of Hailsham.

Kathy becomes Ruth's carer. There is **tension** between them, which worries Kathy.

Ruth asks Kathy to take her to see a deserted boat that has washed up in a marsh along the coast. The boat happens to be near Kingsfield, the **recovery centre** where Tommy is. They agree to pick him up so that they can all see the boat together.

Chapter 19 describes their trip to the boat. During their walk to the boat, Ruth's fragility is highlighted. Kathy realises that Ruth has changed considerably.

On the drive home, Ruth asks Tommy and Kathy for forgiveness. She admits to keeping the pair apart. She provides them with Madame's address and tells them to ask for a deferral.

Kathy is reluctant to accept Ruth's advice, and continues to care for Ruth. Their relationship improves. However, Ruth **completes** after her second donation. In their last conversation, Kathy agrees to care for Tommy.

Finally, in Chapter 20, Kathy becomes Tommy's carer and they start a sexual relationship. Kathy expresses regret for waiting so long.

Tommy shares his artwork with Kathy. Again, she feels that it may be too late, but she does not tell Tommy. They make plans to visit Madame after Kathy discovers that the address is real.

What is the importance of the boat?

The boat in Chapter 19 is a strong source of **imagery**. It represents the students themselves – it is abandoned and falling apart. Kathy describes how the timber frames are showing and that the once sky blue paint has faded to almost white.

This is comparable to the descriptions of Ruth and Tommy, who themselves are being taken apart, bit by bit, through their donations. For example, while walking, Ruth's breath came 'less and less easily' and Kathy is shocked when she notices 'just how frail' she had become. Tommy is also described as having 'a limp in his gait'.

Kathy also describes how Ruth is no longer as opinionated or bossy as she once was. Again, she is 'bothered' by how Ruth had 'just taken it' and had not '[struck] back' at Tommy and Kathy when they had 'ganged up' on her in the car. Instead, her 'eyes looked far away, fixed to somewhere on the sky'.

How is Ruth presented in this section of the text?

Ruth is weak and frail. She does not argue with Kathy as much as she used to, often sitting in silent contemplation.

She shows remorse for her past behaviour, especially towards Kathy and Tommy. She admits to telling lies in the past.

When she completes after her second donation, this is meant to be quite tragic, as Kathy says it does not happen often.

Key Quotations to Learn

And it was then, as she stood there, her shoulders rising and falling with her breathing, that Tommy seemed to become aware for the first time just how frail she was. (Kathy: Chapter 19)

'The main thing is, I kept you and Tommy apart.' (Ruth: Chapter 19)

So that feeling came again, even though I tried to keep it out: that we were doing all of this too late; that there'd once been a time for it, but we'd let that go by, and there was something ridiculous, reprehensible even, about the way we were now thinking and planning. (Kathy: Chapter 20)

Summary

- Kathy becomes Ruth's carer.
- Ruth asks Kathy to organise a trip to visit Tommy and view the abandoned boat.
- Ruth apologises for keeping Kathy and Tommy apart; she gives them Madame's address and tells them they should try for a deferral.
- Ruth completes.
- Kathy becomes Tommy's carer; they plan to go and see Madame.

Questions

QUICK TEST
1. What happened to Hailsham?
2. Where does Ruth ask Kathy to take her?
3. What does Ruth admit to Kathy and Tommy?
4. Why does Ruth give Kathy Madame's address?
5. Why does Kathy become Tommy's carer?

EXAM PRACTICE
Using one or more of the 'Key Quotations to Learn', write about how the writer builds tension in the text.

Part Three (Chapters 21 to 23)

You must be able to: understand what happens in the second half of Part Three.

What happens?

In Chapter 21, Tommy and Kathy drive to Madame's address. Madame invites them in and they explain why they have come. Madame asks many questions, but does not provide any answers.

Miss Emily appears in Chapter 22 and explains that the deferral rumours are not true. She attempts to explain what they were trying to accomplish at Hailsham, but says that the world was not ready to see the students as human.

Miss Emily suggests the students should feel lucky; Hailsham gave them a childhood that other students – or **clones**, as the rest of the world views them – do not receive.

Tommy asks about Miss Lucy and finds out she was fired because she was too **idealistic**; she disagreed with what the students were told about their futures. Miss Emily wanted to keep the students sheltered, while Miss Lucy wanted them to be told the truth about their existence.

As they are leaving, Kathy asks Madame about the time she saw her dancing. Madame admits that she wept because she knew Kathy would never get to live a full life.

In Chapter 23, Tommy asks Kathy to get him a new carer – he doesn't want her to see him suffer in the lead up to his fourth donation. Kathy leaves Tommy at Kingsfield. She does not see him again and finds out that he completed after his fourth donation.

Kathy drives to Norfolk shortly after she finds out about Tommy's completion. She imagines seeing him wave at her in the distance.

How is Madame presented in this section of the text?

Madame invites Tommy and Kathy into her house. She is not warm towards them, but much of the revulsion Kathy saw previously is gone.

Madame listens calmly to what Kathy and Tommy have to say. She appears **sympathetic**, often shaking her head and expressing sadness.

When Miss Emily takes over the conversation, Madame retreats. Miss Emily explains that Madame has always been on the students' side.

Madame explains that when she saw Kathy dancing alone as a young girl it broke her heart.

As Kathy and Tommy leave, Madame touches Kathy's face and expresses sadness over what has happened.

Key Quotations to Learn

'We took away your art because we thought it would reveal your souls. Or to put it more finely, we did it to *prove you had souls at all.*' (Miss Emily: Chapter 22)

'No, Tommy. There's nothing like that. Your life must now run the course that's been set for it.' (Miss Emily: Chapter 22)

'Very well, sometimes that meant we kept things from you, lied to you. Yes, in many ways we *fooled* you. I suppose you could even call it that. But we sheltered you during those years, and we gave you your childhoods.' (Miss Emily: Chapter 22)

Summary

- Miss Emily explains that deferrals are just a rumour – there is no escaping their **fate**.
- The students find out that their artwork was taken to prove that they had souls.
- Tommy asks Kathy for a new carer: shortly after, he completes.
- Kathy continues with her duties as a carer.

Questions

QUICK TEST
1. What do Kathy and Tommy learn about deferrals?
2. Why was Miss Lucy fired?
3. When does Tommy complete?

EXAM PRACTICE
Using one or more of the 'Key Quotations to Learn', write about the character of Miss Emily.

Narrative Structure

You must be able to: explain the significance of how Ishiguro has structured the text.

How does the plot unfold?

The narrator of the text is Kathy H. Throughout the text, she looks back on her life, across three distinct stages.

Part One is at Hailsham, where Kathy describes her childhood, between the ages of 11 and 16.

Part Two is at the Cottages, and is an in-between stage for the students, before they start caring. Kathy is at the Cottages for a year or two.

Part Three takes place seven years later, when Kathy is a carer, in various recovery centres around England.

However, the events in each chapter are not necessarily **chronological**: Kathy often jumps from one memory to another, reflecting realistic thought patterns. As such, her narration is **non-linear**.

What kind of narrator is Kathy?

Kathy is a conversational, **first person narrator**. She speaks using **colloquial** language. She is somewhat unreliable, as she often admits she might not remember things exactly as they happened. We only see things from her point of view.

Kathy addresses the reader using **direct address**, as if the reader is also a carer.

Kathy only ever refers to others like her as students, not clones. Her language is very clinical in some regards, suggesting she accepts her position in society. For example, she says 'Just now and then you run into a student you know – a carer or donor you recognise from the old days'.

A key feature in her narration is **foreshadowing**: Kathy often talks about something happening before she describes it to the reader. This is evident in Chapter 4 when she says 'I realise now just how much of what occurred later came out of our time at Hailsham'. In this example, Kathy hints at trouble to come in the future, but explains how she must first look in detail at the past in order to make what happens later seem more **poignant**.

How does Ishiguro reveal information about the students' purpose?

Ishiguro is able to slowly reveal the reality of the students' lives. In Chapter 1 Kathy describes being a carer and mentions donors as if the reader should have prior knowledge of these terms: 'If you're one of them [a carer], I can understand how you'd get resentful [about her boasting]'.

Kathy's conversational tone emphasises her acceptance of her way of life as normal; she expects the reader to have had similar experiences. For example, Kathy says 'I don't know how it was where you were, but at Hailsham we had to have some form of medical almost every week'.

However, the reality of their lives is not made explicit until Miss Lucy gives her speech in chapter 7. It isn't until after this moment that things start to become clearer to the reader.

Key Quotations to Learn

There have been times over the years when I've tried to leave Hailsham behind, when I've told myself I shouldn't look back so much. But then there came a point when I just stopped resisting. (Kathy: Chapter 1)

This was all a long time ago so I may have some of it wrong … (Kathy: Chapter 2)

What I've got today isn't the actual cassette, the one I had back then at Hailsham, the one I lost. It's the one Tommy and I found in Norfolk years afterwards – but that's another story I'll come to later. (Kathy: Chapter 6)

You'll have heard the same talk. (Kathy: Chapter 23)

Summary

- Kathy is the only narrator.
- The structure is non-linear – it does not necessarily flow chronologically.
- The plot takes place across three parts, each representing a distinct phase in Kathy's life.
- Ishiguro carefully reveals information about Kathy's existence throughout the text.
- Kathy often foreshadows things that will later happen in the text.

Questions

QUICK TEST
1. What type of narrator is Kathy?
2. What three sections is the novel split into?
3. What makes the narration non-linear?

EXAM PRACTICE
Using one or more of the 'Key Quotations to Learn', write about how Ishiguro presents Kathy as a narrator.

Kazuo Ishiguro and Cloning

You must be able to: understand how the novel's meaning has been shaped by the author's life and the time in which he was writing.

Who is Kazuo Ishiguro?

Kazuo Ishiguro was born in Nagasaki, Japan, in 1954. His parents were alive during the Second World War and the bombing of Japan, but he says he was sheltered from talk of war by his parents. He moved to Britain when he was five years old.

This sheltered experience of growing up is evident in the students of Hailsham; Miss Emily fires Miss Lucy when she attempts to tell the students the truth about their existence.

Ishiguro was educated at a grammar school in Surrey, later studying English and Philosophy at the University of Kent. He began writing full-time in 1982. His experiences in grammar school may have influenced his depiction of Hailsham, which is modelled on an alternative private school system, with clones boarding at their place of education.

Philosophy is the study of general and fundamental problems concerning matters such as existence, knowledge, values, reason, the mind and language; these topics all have their place within *Never Let Me Go*.

How does the time the novel was written affect the text?

The text was written at a time when **cloning** was becoming a reality. The first successful cloning of an animal, Dolly the sheep, occurred in 1996. This provided scientific proof that cloning was possible and it caused a lot of controversy around the implications it may have for human cloning.

The first successful human clone was created in 1998, although the **embryo** was destroyed.

These views are presented in the text through Miss Emily and Madame. In Chapter 22, Miss Emily describes how 'after the war' the clones were nothing more than 'shadowy objects in test tubes' and that people only wanted to view then as 'medical supply'. She suggests that people would rather avoid controversy by not knowing anything about the clones, because 'there was no way to reverse the progress' made by their creation.

The use of **DNA** to identify people began to be used in criminal law in the 1990s as well.

Embryonic stem cell research, which takes and uses cells from fertilised human eggs, first started in 1998. It continues to cause controversy around the world.

The first **gene therapy** trials (being able to pick and choose characteristics for your children) also started in the 1990s. Again, Miss Emily mentions this advancement in the novel when she describes the 'Morningdale scandal': here, Ishiguro presents us with controversial scientist James Morningdale, who began to create embryos with 'enhanced characteristics'.

Miss Emily describes a huge public backlash against this type of science, suggesting there was fear over creating 'children who'd take the place of naturally born children'.

Many countries around the world have outlawed human cloning. The idea of human cloning remains controversial. In the text, Ishiguro suggests that a 'donation programme', such as the one in the novel, could be allowed to exist, as long as people are not forced to 'think about [the clones] or about the conditions [they are] brought up in'.

Summary

- Kazuo Ishiguro was born in Japan but grew up in Britain. He attended grammar school and studied philosophy at university.
- Medical science, particularly the ability to clone, expanded in the 1990s.
- Issues around human cloning remain controversial today.

Questions

QUICK TEST
1. How could Ishiguro's childhood and education have influenced parts of the text?
2. How do Miss Emily's views of cloning fit in with modern views?
3. What philosophical issues does Ishiguro present in the novel?

EXAM PRACTICE
In Chapter 22, Miss Emily says:
'And for a long time, people preferred to believe these organs appeared from nowhere, or at most that they grew in a kind of vacuum. Yes, there *were* arguments. But by the time people became concerned about … about *students* … well by then it was too late.'

Relating your ideas to the book's contemporary context, write a paragraph explaining how Miss Emily's views might reflect Ishiguro's views about cloning.

Technology in the Novel

You must be able to: link the events of the text to its setting.

How is modern technology used in the novel?

The 1990s are often seen as a time when the media and technology grew. Cable television became more widespread and the internet became increasingly commonplace in homes and businesses. Early cell phones were available, although they were not widely used.

Interestingly, these types of technology are not mentioned by Kathy, aside from television. Even then, Kathy says that 'Television at Hailsham had been pretty restricted' and that even at the Cottages 'no one was very keen on it'. This suggests that the clones lived a very sheltered life.

This adds to the sense of isolation Ishiguro creates; while the clones co-exist with members of the public, they are on the fringes and are kept largely separate. They are unable to communicate with each other except through face-to-face encounters or word of mouth, despite significant improvements in communication technology at the time.

When they do watch television, they use it to emulate social cues: Kathy describes how she 'began to notice' how the veterans copied things like 'the way they gestured to each other, sat together on sofas, even the way they argued' from television shows.

In the 1990s there was an increase in companies and the media marketing products specifically at young people, such as fashion, music, television and so on. However, these types of fads are largely ignored by Kathy and her friends. Unlike other, 'normal', teenagers, they seem unconcerned with things like fashion, music and celebrity.

Interestingly, Miss Emily, in Chapter 22, describes how 'that awful television programme' contributed to the change in public perception about clones. This suggests a programme was created centring on the lives of clones, likely depicting them in a way she found unfavourable to her cause.

Music of the 1990s saw the rise of grunge, punk, electronic dance music, rap and hip-hop, as well as pop bands such as the Spice Girls and Take That. In the United Kingdom, a new form of 'Britpop' culture emerged; this included bands such as Blur, Oasis and The Verve.

Music would have been available on cassette tapes or compact discs, which were the most current format for storing and listening to music, although MP3 players became more widespread towards the end of the decade. Portable music players, such as the Walkman, became popular items for teens during the 1990s. Kathy herself mentions a Walkman in Chapter 6, although this is in reference to her not being able to have one to herself. Again, this highlights the lack of personal possessions, and access to modern technology, afforded to the clones.

In the novel, the only mention of music is reflected in the title: Kathy's (fictional) Judy Bridgewater *Never Let Me Go* tape. She describes the Bridgewater tape as 'cocktail-bar stuff', not popular with others her age. Ruth also gets her a tape of 'orchestra stuff for ballroom dancing', which she was 'disappointed' with, but later came to love for its sentimental value.

Summary

- Technology, such as the internet and cable television, became more widespread in the 1990s. However, this was not made available to the clones.
- Advances in communication technology were denied to the clones; they had to communicate face to face, or via word of mouth.
- The clones only watch television to learn social cues from it, not necessarily for entertainment value.

Questions

QUICK TEST
1. Why could providing the clones with things like the internet and television be dangerous?
2. Why would the clones want to emulate behaviour seen on television?
3. How does Ishiguro use the lack of technology in the novel to highlight the clones' isolation?

EXAM PRACTICE
Consider this passage from Part 1:

But the reason the tape meant so much to me had nothing to do with the cigarette, or even with the way Judy Bridgewater sang – she's one of those singers from her time, cocktail-bar stuff, not the sort of thing any of us at Hailsham liked …

… I didn't have many opportunities, mind you, this being a few years before Walkman started appearing at the Sales.

Relating your ideas to the historical context, write a paragraph explaining how Kathy's experience growing up in the 1990s was realistic for that time period.

You must be able to: understand how Kathy is presented throughout the text.

What is Kathy like?

Kathy is the narrator of the novel. She is 31 years old when she begins the story and is working as a carer.

Kathy is proud of her role of carer. She says that she has 'developed a kind of instinct around donors' that allows her to gauge when they need comforting and when they need time alone. Her success as a carer shows how compassionate she is.

However, she acknowledges how tough the job can be, suggesting that she pushes her own emotions aside. Due to her successes, she has been able to choose who she cares for. This is a rare privilege among carers: she says she's 'not the first to be allowed to pick and choose' and she doubts she'll 'be the last'.

She often looks out for Tommy, expressing sympathy for him when he is bullied by others. In Chapter 1, she goes to help him, 'even when [she] heard Ruth's urgent whisper … to come back'.

She is also very **tolerant** of Ruth; she can sometimes be quite **passive**. She sticks up for Ruth often, despite Ruth not always being kind to her. For example, when Ruth looks to Tommy and Kathy for support with Chrissie and Rodney, Tommy refuses to agree, but Kathy says 'You know, Tommy. All that talk that used to go around Hailsham' in an attempt to save Ruth embarrassment.

She also allows Ruth to **manipulate** her into doing things, such as helping bring Tommy and Ruth back together or even agreeing to become Tommy's carer.

However, she is also very headstrong and determined. When leaving the Cottages, she says 'once I'd made [up my mind], I never wavered'. More examples of this determination include outing Ruth for lying about Miss Geraldine and the pencil case, becoming Ruth's and then Tommy's carer and going to Madame regarding a deferral.

How does Kathy view herself?

Hailsham had a large effect on Kathy – she remains tied to Hailsham throughout the novel. Most of her **reminiscences** can be linked back to Hailsham in some way. It bothers her when people forget things that happened at Hailsham.

Kathy struggles with her identity throughout the text. She often doubts her own actions and thoughts. For example, she feels that her sexual urges are not normal and she struggles to have long-term relationships with boys.

However, Kathy is accepting of her fate. Neither she nor Tommy argue with Miss Emily when she tells them there are no deferrals. She continues to do her job, up until the very end of the novel.

Key Quotations to Learn

My donors have always tended to do much better than expected. Their recovery times have been impressive, and hardly any of them have been classified as 'agitated', even before a fourth donation. Okay, maybe I *am* boasting now. (Kathy: Chapter 1)

And then there was the way Ruth kept pretending to forget things about Hailsham. Okay, these were mostly trivial things, but I got more and more irritated with her. (Kathy: Chapter 16)

The memories I value most, I don't see them ever fading. I lost Ruth, then I lost Tommy, but I won't lose my memories of them. (Kathy: Chapter 23)

Summary

- Kathy is kind and caring – she is good at her job of caring for donors.
- Her relationship with Ruth is one of both admiration and irritation; however, overall, she feels great love towards her.
- Her relationship with Tommy was always caring – when they finally become a couple it feels as if they had waited too long.
- She has strong, positive memories of her time at Hailsham.
- She accepts her fate and does not rebel against it.

Sample Analysis

Kathy puts aside her personal feelings for Tommy in order to be a good friend to Ruth. For example, when Ruth asks for her help getting back together with Tommy, she is initially disappointed. When Ruth asks 'What's the matter?', her response suggests a **dramatic pause**; she says 'Nothing. I'm just a bit surprised'. Her use of the **noun** 'Nothing' emphasises how she's not only trying to convince Ruth, but herself, that it's a good idea. Later in the chapter, she **pauses** again before asking Ruth if she's 'serious about Tommy', showing her concern for both of them and, to some extent, herself.

Questions

QUICK TEST
1. What privileges does Kathy suggest she has as an adult?
2. How does she feel about Hailsham?
3. How does Kathy feel about her future/fate?

EXAM PRACTICE
Using one or more quotes from the 'Key Quotations to Learn', write a paragraph analysing how Ishiguro presents Kathy's sense of self.

You must be able to: understand how Ruth is presented throughout the text.

How is Ruth presented as manipulative?

Ruth and Kathy first become friends at Hailsham. However, Kathy soon catches on to Ruth's manipulative nature. Ruth cuts Kathy out of their secret guard when Kathy begins to question her stories about Miss Geraldine. Kathy describes how 'it suddenly hit me what was about to happen' and how she 'felt the hurt even before they went silent and stared' at her.

Ruth is determined to stay with Tommy. She convinces Kathy to help her with Tommy and repeatedly twists Kathy's words to criticise and humiliate him. For example, she tells Tommy that Kathy 'finds [his] animals a complete hoot', which causes tension between Kathy and Tommy.

How is Ruth shown to lack self-esteem?

At Hailsham, Ruth tells lies to put herself in a position of power over others. When Kathy confronts her about lying about the pencil case, her 'loss for words' and appearing 'on the verge of tears' show that while she appears hard on the outside, inside she struggles with her own identity.

At the Cottages, Ruth is desperate to fit in. Here, Kathy describes there being 'two quite separate Ruths'. When Kathy confronts Ruth in Chapter 10 about her behaviour, she reacts angrily. Kathy describes how a 'gleam c[a]me into [her] eyes' when she said 'that's what's upsetting poor little Kathy'. She goes on to say that Ruth 'was struggling to become someone else, and maybe felt more pressure than the rest of us'.

Ruth takes many of her social cues from those around her. When she sees that other veterans are not openly affectionate, she quickly changes her own behaviour. Kathy describes not liking the Ruth she 'could see every day putting on airs and pretending'.

She also copies behaviour seen on television, which Kathy finds ridiculous. However, on reflection, Kathy admits (in Chapter 11) that she 'never appreciated ... the sheer effort Ruth was making to move on, to grow up and leave Hailsham behind'.

How does Ishiguro reveal that Ruth is a believer?

Both Tommy and Kathy describe Ruth as a believer – someone who hoped for a better outcome.

Ruth entertains ideas of one day working in an office. In Chapter 12, she tells the other students 'about the sort of office she'd ideally work in'. The **adverb** 'ideally' emphasises her idealistic nature. When Rodney indicates he may have found her possible in an office in Cromer, she can barely contain her excitement: 'she was completely set on going'.

However, Ruth is extremely let down when the woman is not her possible; she lashes out at Tommy and Kathy. She aggressively tells Tommy to 'shut up' and says that Kathy 'never likes straight talking'.

It is Ruth who finds Madame's address – she is convinced that Tommy and Kathy can get a deferral and regrets her intervention in their relationship. She repeats that it 'was the worst thing' she did and feels that they have a 'real chance' at getting a deferral.

Key Quotations to Learn

'Tommy and I were made for each other and he'll listen to you. You'll do it for us, won't you, Kathy?' (Ruth: Chapter 9)

'It's not just me, sweety. Kathy here finds your animals a complete hoot.' (Ruth: Chapter 16)

'It should have been you two. I'm not pretending I didn't always see that. Of course I did, as far back as I can remember. But I kept you apart.' (Ruth: Chapter 19)

Summary

- Ruth is manipulative – she likes to be in control.
- She intentionally keeps Tommy and Kathy apart, although she comes to regret this.
- She believes Kathy and Tommy have a chance for a deferral and, to make up for past mistakes, she provides them with Madame's address.

Sample Analysis

Ruth is presented as bossy. Even as a young child, she controlled Kathy when playing with her imaginary horses. When she approaches Kathy, she says that she's 'not to use [her] crop on [Bramble]. And you've got to come *now*'. She uses **imperative** verbs such as 'come *now*' and 'ride them here' to show **dominance** over Kathy. Kathy is surprised when Ruth 'suddenly, for no reason I could see' stops the game claiming that Kathy 'deliberately' tired out the horses. These adverbs show that Ruth acts unpredictably in order to remain in control.

Questions

QUICK TEST
1. In what ways does Ruth manipulate others?
2. Why does she keep Kathy and Tommy apart?
3. What sort of future does Ruth hope for?

EXAM PRACTICE
Using one or more of the 'Key Quotations to Learn', write a paragraph analysing how Ishiguro presents Ruth in different parts of the novel.

You must be able to: understand how Tommy is presented throughout the text.

How is Tommy presented at the beginning of the novel?

Tommy is a figure of pity and interest for Kathy. She describes how girls were 'gathered around the windows' to watch 'Tommy get humiliated yet again'. Later, Kathy tells us that others think he 'brought it upon himself' and that his temper led to him being 'left out of games'.

Tommy and Kathy develop a close friendship that carries on throughout the novel. Tommy confides in Kathy, showing he trusts her.

At Hailsham, Tommy struggles with art. This is important because 'how much you were liked and respected, had to do with how good you were at "creating"', which works against Tommy. Initially, Miss Lucy tells him it is okay not to be creative.

However, when Miss Lucy changes her mind this causes him distress. He feels he may have missed an important opportunity by failing to be creative. He admits that it is 'not a game any more', showing that he's beginning to take his creativity more seriously.

Tommy views the world very literally. He is often left out of jokes and does not follow along when Ruth lies to others. For example, he embarrasses Ruth by saying 'I don't know what you're all talking about. What rules are these?'.

Despite having a connection with Kathy, Tommy goes out with Ruth. However, even before leaving Hailsham Tommy seems dubious about their future: he says that he doesn't want to 'rush back into it with Ruth' because 'We've got to think about the next move really carefully'.

At the Cottages, their relationship does not seem strong. Tommy confides more in Kathy, which makes Ruth jealous. This foreshadows their eventual breakup and, indeed, when they leave the Cottages to become carers, their relationship ends.

What is Tommy like at the end of the novel?

Tommy is presented as a strong, forgiving character. When re-introduced to Kathy, we learn he has made it through three donations. Kathy and Tommy are able to 'come close together again after all the years'.

He holds no grudge against Ruth. Kathy describes how 'his voice was full of child-like curiosity' when he speaks after Ruth's confession. He accepts Madame's address and 'solemnly' thanks Ruth.

Tommy and Kathy start a relationship after Ruth completes. Kathy also becomes his carer. He expresses regret that it took them so long. At the start of Chapter 20, Kathy describes how 'there was something in Tommy's manner that was tinged with sadness'.

Tommy is also very proud. He asks Kathy to find him a new carer because he doesn't want her to see him in pain. He shows concern that she not 'take this the wrong way', but ultimately, he doesn't 'want to be that way in front' of her.

Key Quotations to Learn

'Funny thing is […] it did help.' (Tommy: Chapter 3)

'... even though Tommy was at Hailsham, he isn't like a real Hailsham student.' (Ruth: Chapter 13)

'So, what you're saying, Miss […] is that everything we did, all the lessons, everything. It was all about what you just told us? There was nothing more to it than that?' (Tommy: Chapter 22)

Summary

- Tommy had a bad temper as a child. This caused him to be bullied.
- He was not very creative as a child, and regrets this as he gets older.
- He finally has a relationship with Kathy, but only after Ruth has died.
- He is hopeful for a deferral with Kathy, and is disappointed when it turns out to be a rumour.
- He completes on his own, without Kathy's help.

Sample Analysis

Tommy is presented as someone who struggles to control his temper. For example, at the beginning of the novel, Ishiguro lists **verbs** such as 'raving, flinging his limbs about' when describing one of his temper tantrums. This behaviour is mirrored towards the end of the novel, when he asks Kathy to pull over after their visit to see Madame. Again, Ishiguro uses a list of verbs such as 'raging, shouting, flinging his fists and kicking out' to show how, despite all this time passing, Tommy still struggles to control his anger.

Questions

QUICK TEST
1. Why do the Hailsham students pick on Tommy?
2. Why does Tommy worry about his creativity?
3. How and why does Tommy change throughout the novel?

EXAM PRACTICE
Using one or more of the 'Key Quotations to Learn', write a paragraph analysing how Ishiguro presents Tommy at different points in the novel.

You must be able to: understand how Miss Lucy is presented throughout the text.

How does Ishiguro present Miss Lucy in Part One?

Miss Lucy is a well-liked guardian. She often speaks about the future with the students. She leaves the school amidst mysterious circumstances.

Tommy describes how Miss Lucy spoke to him at length about his lack of creativity. Initially, she told him that creativity wasn't something he should worry about.

Miss Lucy is described as 'Shaking. With rage.' throughout her conversation with Tommy. She tells Tommy that the students are 'not being taught enough' about 'what's going to happen to [them] one day', showing how passionate she was about providing students with the basic facts about their existence.

However, Miss Lucy later changes her mind about Tommy's creativity. She tells him that she 'made a mistake' and had 'done [him] a big disservice telling [him] not to worry about being creative'. She asks him to continue creating artwork, 'for [his] own sake', and because it is valuable 'evidence'.

Despite wanting to tell the students the truth, her conversations with Tommy reveal a cautious approach. While it is clear she wants to say more, she holds herself back from saying anything truly incriminating, instead suggesting that 'one day' he will figure out the truth. Ishiguro uses Miss Lucy to foreshadow Tommy's quest for truth later in the novel because she suggests that there are ways for him to find out the truth.

Miss Lucy suddenly leaves Hailsham. Her departure is shocking to the students: the news of her leaving 'spread through [the students] in an instant'. The reader later learns that she was fired by Miss Emily for being too idealistic.

How does Ishiguro present Miss Lucy in Part Three?

Miss Lucy comes up again when Tommy and Kathy visit Madame and Miss Emily.

Towards the end of their visit, Tommy asks what happened to Miss Lucy. Miss Emily is dismissive of her at first; she says 'we had a little trouble with her' twice, emphasising the difficulties Miss Lucy caused for Miss Emily.

However, after being prompted for more information, Miss Emily says she had to go because she 'began to have these ideas' about making the students more aware of who, or what, they were. According to Miss Emily, '[s]he believed you should be given as full a picture as possible' and that not doing so was to 'cheat' the students.

It is clear that Miss Lucy disagreed with how things were done at Hailsham and that Miss Emily was not willing to change. Tommy later suggests that Miss Lucy's way of thinking would have been more beneficial than Miss Emily's; he says 'I think Miss Lucy was right. Not Miss Emily'.

Key Quotations to Learn

'Shaking. With rage. I could see her. She was furious. But furious deep inside.' (Tommy: Chapter 3)

'The problem, as I see it, is that you've been told and not told. You've been told, but none of you really understand, and I dare say, some people are quite happy to leave it that way. But I'm not.' (Miss Lucy: Chapter 7)

'But perhaps one day, you'll try and find out. They won't make it easy for you, but if you really want to, really want to, you might find out.' (Miss Lucy: Chapter 9)

Summary

- Miss Lucy is a young guardian who speaks honestly with the students about their future.
- She tells Tommy that it is okay to not be creative, but later changes her mind.
- She is fired because she is too idealistic.

Sample Analysis

Miss Lucy's anger is clear when she 'turned to face' the students and 'spoke loudly' about how talk of the future 'has been allowed to go on, and it's not right'. The verb 'allowed' suggests something has been permitted and the **adjectival phrase** 'not right' shows her disagreement with the rules. These contrasting statements highlight Miss Lucy's anger with how the students are taught at Hailsham.

Questions

QUICK TEST
1. What information does Miss Lucy provide to Tommy?
2. Why does Miss Lucy tell Tommy to continue making artwork?
3. Why was Miss Lucy fired from Hailsham?

EXAM PRACTICE
Using one or more of the 'Key Quotations to Learn', write about the role of Miss Lucy in the novel.

You must be able to: understand how Miss Emily is presented throughout the text.

Who is Miss Emily and what was her role at Hailsham?

Miss Emily was head guardian. The students 'were all pretty scared of her' but they 'considered her to be fair and respected her decisions'. She is an intimidating character who commands respect. Interestingly, Kathy says that she 'wasn't especially tall, but something about the way she carried herself … made you think she was'. Ishiguro creates this imagery around Miss Emily to emphasise the strength of her beliefs and power over the students of Hailsham.

She is presented as strict, lecturing the students on how they must be careful. For example, in Chapter 4, Kathy describes how she would 'order us to sit down on the floor', where she'd spend 'twenty, thirty minutes' lecturing them. While she'd 'rarely raise her voice' there was 'something steely about her on these occasions'.

Later, the reader learns that she started Hailsham as an experiment. She wanted to raise the profile of clones, showing the world that they deserved more humane treatment.

As head guardian, she controlled what the students were taught. She felt she should protect the students from the realities of their lives; later she defends her decision to 'shelter' the students, going so far as to admit that she 'fooled' them. However, she feels in doing so 'we gave you your childhoods'. Here, Ishiguro has Miss Emily use a range of verbs to justify her decision to lie to the students, something she repeatedly does.

How does Miss Emily feel about the students of Hailsham?

While Miss Emily wants to affect change for clones, it is clear that she is uncomfortable around them. She admits that sometimes she would 'look down at [the students] from [her] study window and […] feel such revulsion'.

She suggests that Hailsham failed because the 'world didn't want to be reminded how the donation programme really worked', suggesting that people would rather remain ignorant.

However, this does not detract from her commitment; it is suggested that she has given everything to the cause – for example, men arrive to take away a 'beautiful object' that she is 'determined to get a fair price' for, suggesting that Miss Emily and Madame are still in debt from their work.

She also suggests that Kathy and Tommy should be grateful. She calls them 'lucky pawns' and says that they should just 'accept that sometimes that's how things happen in this world'.

Ultimately, Miss Emily accepts that nothing will change, despite her hard work. She pities Kathy and Tommy, but can do nothing to help them. She offers no apology, despite being sympathetic. Interestingly, her final words to Tommy and Kathy are that she 'was determined not to let such feelings [of revulsion] stop her from doing what was right'.

Key Quotations to Learn

We were all pretty scared of her and didn't think of her in the way we did the other guardians. (Kathy: Chapter 4)

'I don't feel so badly about it. I think what we achieved merits some respect.'
(Miss Emily: Chapter 22)

'You wouldn't be who you are today if we'd not protected you.' (Miss Emily: Chapter 22)

Summary

- Miss Emily was the stern head guardian at Hailsham.

- She set up Hailsham as an experiment, campaigning for better treatment and living conditions for clones.

- She has to let Tommy and Kathy down by telling them there is no hope; they must become donors too. She offers no apology for misleading them.

- Despite her personal repulsion towards the clones, she dedicated much of her life to trying to improve their living conditions.

Sample Analysis

Miss Emily is passionate about Hailsham. She blames other things, such as the Morningdale scandal, for the failure of Hailsham. She creates a **metaphor** of Hailsham as a 'shining beacon' and describes it as 'more humane' than other facilities. She says that Hailsham 'educated' and 'cultured' the students and that they should 'appreciate' what they could 'secure' for them. These verbs highlight the proud view she has of Hailsham.

Questions

QUICK TEST
1. Why did Miss Emily create Hailsham?
2. How does Miss Emily feel about what they accomplished at Hailsham?
3. How does Miss Emily feel towards Tommy and Kathy?

EXAM PRACTICE
Using one or more of the 'Key Quotations to Learn', write about how Ishiguro uses Miss Emily to explore the role of Hailsham.

Madame – Marie Claude

You must be able to: understand how Madame is presented throughout the text.

How is Madame presented in Part One?

Madame came to Hailsham to collect the students' artwork. She would turn up 'twice – sometimes three or four times – each year to select from our best work'. Getting your artwork selected for the Gallery was a point of pride: 'If you wanted to praise someone's work you'd say: "That's good enough for the Gallery"'.

Madame, and her 'Gallery', was a source of curiosity. There was an 'unspoken rule' that students should never ask the guardians about it.

In Chapter 3, six students, including Kathy and Ruth, plan to wait for Madame. They want to test whether Ruth's theory – that Madame is afraid of them – is correct.

Kathy describes how she 'froze and waited for us to pass. She didn't shriek, or even let out a gasp'. Instead, she suppressed a shudder of 'real dread'. Kathy describes how her reaction was similar to 'someone who might be afraid of spiders'. The metaphors used to describe her reaction suggest that Madame was indeed afraid of the students.

How does Madame react when Tommy and Kathy confront her in Part Three?

Madame is not surprised when Tommy and Kathy appear. Again, using imagery of spiders, Kathy describes how 'you could see her stiffen – as if a pair of large spiders was set to crawl towards her'. However, 'something changed in her expression', suggesting that this has happened before.

She listens quietly while Kathy explains why they've come, asking probing questions, such as 'You say you're *sure*?' and 'You believe this? That you're deeply in love?' Her questions show a very **cynical** side to her character – she cannot understand what the students want and is wary of their motives.

However, although Kathy describes her tone of voice as 'almost sarcastic', she also has 'little' tears in her eyes. The contrasting adjectives used here show the reader a more tender side to her character.

Madame offers very little information to Kathy and Tommy. She appears quite cold, detached and clinical. For example, Kathy says '[t]here was something odd about her manner, like she hadn't really invited us to sit down'. She also describes how she 'tucked her shoulders in tightly as she passed between us', showing a physical revulsion to the students, similar to Chapter 3.

Once Miss Emily takes over the conversation, Madame retreats. She occasionally interjects, offering comments about how they let the students down. It is clear she feels they should be more thankful.

Miss Emily admits that Madame took their artwork to prove the students had souls, and suggests that she 'has given *everything*' for them and that she 'is on [their] side and will always be on [their] side'.

As Tommy and Kathy go to leave, Madame apologies. She says that their 'stories touched' her and she repeatedly calls them 'poor creatures'. She expresses regret and sympathy, gently placing a 'trembling' hand on Kathy's face.

Key Quotations to Learn

... there are people out there, like Madame, who don't hate you or wish you any harm, but who nevertheless shudder at the thought of you. (Kathy: Chapter 3)

'You believe this? That you're deeply in love?' (Madame: Chapter 22)

'Poor creatures. What did we do to you? With all our schemes and plans?' (Madame: Chapter 22)

'Why should they be grateful? They came here looking for something much more.' (Madame: Chapter 22)

Summary

- Madame is initially a mysterious figure who comes to take artwork from Hailsham.
- She often expresses fear and revulsion towards the students.
- She expresses regret for the failure of Hailsham.

Sample Analysis

Ishiguro makes it clear that Madame is still scared of Kathy and Tommy. She 'spun around like I'd thrown something at her'. Kathy describes that 'a chill passed through me, much like the one I'd felt years ago'. The **verb phrases** 'spun around' and 'a chill passed through me' mirror Madame's reaction to the clones in Chapter 3, suggesting that she is, and always has been, afraid of the clones.

Questions

QUICK TEST
1. Why did Madame take the artwork?
2. How does Madame feel about the students?
3. How does Madame feel about what happened at Hailsham?

EXAM PRACTICE
Using one or more of the 'Key Quotations to Learn', write about how Ishiguro presents the changes in Madame's character.

Keffers & Chrissie and Rodney

You must be able to: understand how Keffers and Chrissie and Rodney are presented throughout the text.

What is Keffers's role at the Cottages and how is he presented?

Keffers is a 'grumpy old guy' who looks after the farm at the Cottages. He would turn 'up two or three times a week' to check that everything was okay. Kathy describes how 'he didn't like to talk to us much' and that he 'went round sighing and shaking his head disgustedly'. He brings supplies, such as food and fuel, but he 'wouldn't bring many in'.

He is described as repeatedly 'shaking his head' at the students. While the students viewed Keffers as a kind of guardian figure, it is clear that he 'was having none of it'. For him, it was nothing more than a job.

Keffers is also in charge of the students' whereabouts. Kathy describes how they must sign in and out of the Cottages using a ledger: 'no one would stop us if we wandered off, provided we were back by the day and time we entered into Keffers's ledgerbook'.

However, he does have a soft side. When Ruth asks him to donate some of her things to charity, all he did was 'laugh and sa[y] no shop he knew would want stuff like that', but upon seeing Ruth 'getting a bit emotional', he changes his tone, saying 'Now I've had a closer look, you're right, it *is* pretty good stuff'.

He also doesn't allow the students to suffer too much; when 'things were getting really cold' he'd give them 'an envelope with money and a note of some igniter fuel we had to buy', showing that he does have some compassion towards them.

Keffers also starts students on the training process – he provides them with the paperwork needed to get started.

What is the significance of Chrissie and Rodney?

Chrissie and Rodney are a veteran couple who were already at the Cottages when Kathy, Ruth and Tommy arrive.

Kathy quickly realises that Chrissie is in awe of people from Hailsham: 'she was always mentioning the fact that we'd come from Hailsham [...] asking us questions [...] about little details', which Kathy begins to find suspicious.

The way Chrissie and Rodney act has an effect on the other students. Ruth looks to them for social cues, and adapts her behaviour to match theirs. Kathy describes how 'Ruth was making a big effort to present not just herself, but all of us, in the right way', showing just how much their opinion mattered to others.

Rodney is the one who mentions Ruth's possible. When they drive up to see her, the reader soon realises there may be an ulterior motive to the trip. Whilst eating lunch, Chrissie brings up the deferral rumour. She suggests that she heard 'something about Hailsham students in the past' who had 'in special circumstances' received a deferral. Both Rodney and herself look towards the Hailsham students for hope.

Key Quotations to Learn

He didn't like to talk much, and the way he went around sighing and shaking his head disgustedly implied we weren't doing nearly enough to keep the place tidy. (Kathy: Chapter 10)

I suppose Ruth did say a few things every now and then to encourage the idea that, sure enough, in some mysterious way, a separate set of rules applied to us Hailsham students. (Kathy: Chapter 12)

'I know how lucky I am, getting to be at the Cottages. But you Hailsham lot, you're *really* lucky.' (Chrissie: Chapter 13)

Summary

- Keffers is the caretaker at the Cottages.
- He is moody and distant, often muttering under his breath that the students don't do enough around the farm.
- Chrissie idolises people from Hailsham and thinks they get special privileges.
- Chrissie and Rodney are interested in getting a deferral.

Sample Analysis

Chrissie and Rodney are in awe of the Hailsham students, especially Ruth, once they begin to give them information about deferrals. For example, Kathy describes how 'they watched [Ruth] like they were hypnotised', while 'Chrissie looked both afraid and hopeful'. The **simile** 'like they were hypnotised' shows the strong hold Ruth has on them, while the contrasting adjectives 'afraid and hopeful' show how much expectation they are putting on this one conversation.

Questions

QUICK TEST
1. What is Keffers's role at the Cottages?
2. Why does Ruth look up to Chrissie and Rodney?
3. What does Chrissie think of students who come from Hailsham?

EXAM PRACTICE
Using one or more of the 'Key Quotations to Learn', write about how other clones view Hailsham students.

Ruth and Kathy's Relationship

You must be able to: understand how Ishiguro presents the development of the relationship between Kathy and Ruth across the text.

How is the relationship between Kathy and Ruth presented in Part One?

Ruth 'wasn't someone I was friends with from the start', but Kathy was 'absolutely delighted' when Ruth first approached her. Ruth controls much of their play, telling Kathy how to ride the imaginary horses: 'I told you! You've really got to lean back on Daffodil!'.

Ruth prefers to be in control. When Kathy proves Ruth has lied about her experience at chess, Ruth excludes her from the secret guard.

However, Kathy continues to stick up for Ruth. She is surprised at the 'sheer force of the emotion that overtook [her] when [she] heard Moira' insult Ruth. This highlights how eager Kathy is to please Ruth.

Kathy becomes irritated with Ruth's lies. She was 'determined that Ruth shouldn't get away with it' when she catches her lying about the pencil case. However, when she confronts Ruth, she is disappointed in her reaction.

How is the relationship between Kathy and Ruth presented in Part Two?

Kathy describes how 'there were two quite separate Ruths': one 'who was always trying to impress the veterans' and 'the Ruth from Hailsham'. While they were often 'quarrelling over all kinds of little things' they were also 'confiding in each other more than ever'.

Kathy confides in Ruth, particularly about her sexual 'urges'. She is hurt when Ruth throws her confessions back in her face later.

Ruth is jealous of Kathy's relationship with Tommy. When Ruth discovers that Tommy has confided in Kathy, she sabotages their friendship, using Kathy's own words against her: 'It's not just me, sweety. Kathy here finds your animals a complete hoot'.

Later, she tells Kathy that Tommy will never 'see [her] like that' because he 'doesn't like girls who've been with … well, you know, with this person and that', playing on Kathy's fears about her own sexuality. Soon after this, Kathy leaves the Cottages.

The relationship between Kathy and Ruth in Part Three

Kathy and Ruth are reunited when Kathy hears that Ruth's first donation does not go well.

Despite being 'genuinely delighted to be with each other', their relationship becomes tense. Kathy describes 'something not being right' until Ruth mentions visiting the abandoned boat and picking up Tommy.

Here, Ruth asks the pair to forgive her and provides them with Madame's address. She admits to Kathy that she lied to her about her urges, saying that 'I knew how it worried you […] I should have told you […] how it was the same for me'. Ruth shows real maturity and friendship towards Kathy at this point.

Ruth completes soon after. Throughout the text, Kathy reflects on her friendship with Ruth with fond memories. She says that while she 'lost Ruth' she won't 'lose [her] memories' of her. Her death has a big effect on Kathy.

Key Quotations to Learn

And suddenly my behaviour seemed to me utterly baffling. All this effort, all this planning, just to upset my dearest friend. (Kathy: Chapter 5)

I didn't say or do anything. It was partly, I suppose, that I was so floored by the fact that Ruth would come out with such a trick. (Kathy: Chapter 16)

I feel sad she's gone; but I also feel really grateful for that period we had at the end. (Kathy: Chapter 19)

Summary

- Ruth and Kathy have a love/hate relationship.
- Ruth manipulates things to keep Tommy and Kathy apart.
- Before she dies, Ruth asks for forgiveness and tells Kathy and Tommy they should try for a deferral. She gives them Madame's address.

Sample Analysis

After Ruth comes clean to Kathy about her lies in the past, their relationship improves. This is evident when Kathy says 'All the guardedness, all the suspicions between me and Ruth evaporated'. Listing the **abstract nouns** 'guardedness' and 'suspicions' and using the verb 'evaporated' show how being open and honest with each other, after all those years, finally allowed Ruth and Kathy to become friends again.

Questions

QUICK TEST
1. Why does Ruth exclude Kathy from the secret guard at Hailsham?
2. How does Ruth use what Kathy says to sabotage her friendship with Tommy?
3. What does Ruth ask forgiveness for in Part Three?

EXAM PRACTICE
Using one or more of the 'Key Quotations to Learn', write about how Ishiguro presents Kathy's feelings towards Ruth.

Kathy and Tommy's Relationship

You must be able to: understand how Ishiguro presents the development of the relationship between Kathy and Tommy across the text.

How is their relationship presented in Part One?

Kathy looks out for Tommy and tries to help him handle his emotions. She sticks up for him, saying 'it wasn't very fair' how the others picked on him. In return, he confides in her: he says 'I'll tell you Kath, but you mustn't spread it, all right?' showing that he trusts her.

When he starts to go out with Ruth, Kathy focuses on other boys. However, when Ruth and Tommy split up, Kathy becomes confused and 'found [herself] thinking a lot about it'. It is here that she starts to acknowledge her feelings for Tommy.

However, Ruth quickly intervenes. Kathy puts aside her own feelings, despite being 'a bit surprised', to stay on Ruth's good side. However, she doesn't agree to help until Ruth admits to being 'serious about Tommy' and that she 'won't hurt him again', showing her concern for him.

How does their relationship develop in Part Two?

Ruth and Tommy continue to go out with each other at the Cottages. Despite this, Kathy and Tommy continue to have a close friendship.

It isn't until they are left alone in Cromer that their relationship begins to change. The pair spend a nice afternoon together. Kathy describes this afternoon as being full of 'fun and laughter'.

Tommy also confides in Kathy about starting up his drawings again: 'I *have* been doing some stuff. Just in case. I haven't told anyone, not even Ruth'. He shares his theory about Madame's Gallery with Kathy, even before he shares this information with Ruth, suggesting a stronger bond between them.

What is their relationship like at the end of the novel?

After Ruth confesses to keeping them apart, Kathy agrees to become Tommy's carer. They naturally fall into a new kind of relationship, although it is one 'tinged with sadness'. Both regret waiting so long to become a couple.

Before Tommy's fourth donation, they agree to visit Madame and ask for a deferral. Before they set off, Kathy admits to feeling 'that we were doing all of this too late', and goes through with it because Tommy had been trying so hard with his artwork.

They are disappointed when they find out it was nothing more than a rumour. Tommy's reaction is especially distressing. He asks Kathy to stop driving, and then goes into a field where Kathy describes him as 'raging, shouting, flinging his fists and kicking out', reacting much like he did when he was a young, angry boy.

Soon after, Tommy asks Kathy to find him a new carer. He does not want her to see him suffer 'like that'. She leaves him with little fanfare.

Key Quotations to Learn

... I started to drift over towards him. I knew this would puzzle the others, but I kept going – even when I heard Ruth's urgent whisper to me to come back. (Kathy: Chapter 1)

We were just enjoying looking through all those things together; drifting apart then finding ourselves side by side again, (Kathy: Chapter 15)

'I keep thinking about this river somewhere, with the water moving really fast. And these two people in the water, trying to hold on to each other, holding on as hard as they can,' (Tommy: Chapter 23)

Summary

- Kathy and Tommy are friends for much of their lives – Ruth works hard to keep them from becoming lovers.
- They only become a couple after Ruth dies. Both express regret for waiting so long.
- They are both eager to ask for a deferral, eager for more time together, and are disappointed when they find out it is nothing more than a rumour.
- Tommy asks Kathy to find him a new carer. He does not want her to see him die.

Sample Analysis

Kathy describes her last day with Tommy with sadness, but suggests that it was inevitable. For example, she describes how they were 'reluctant to start any new conversation we'd regret not being able to finish' and describes how there was a 'kind of emptiness to [their] talk that day'. She uses verbs such as 'reluctant' and 'regret' to emphasise her sadness. The metaphor 'emptiness to our talk' suggests a cautious sadness associated with their last day together; they want to enjoy their final moments, but fear leaving anything unfinished.

Questions

QUICK TEST
1. Why is Kathy confused when Ruth and Tommy break up at Hailsham?
2. Why is it significant that Tommy buys the cassette for Kathy?
3. What does Ishiguro show about Tommy and Kathy's relationship when he asks for a new carer?

EXAM PRACTICE
Using one or more of the 'Key Quotations to Learn', write about how Ishiguro presents the relationship between Kathy and Tommy in the text.

Identity

You must be able to: analyse how the theme of identity is presented in the text.

What is identity?

In this text, identity refers to the characteristics and influences that make someone who or what they are. Identity can include personal qualities, beliefs, personality and so on. In the text, Ishiguro presents characters who are constantly questioning their identity and place in the world. This is because they are clones with no real awareness of where they come from.

How do the students view their own identity?

At Hailsham, the students develop their own identities through their collections. The items that they accumulate are kept in special wooden chests. In Part Two, Kathy describes how students from other centres did not have these chests.

Currency for the Sales is obtained through creative ventures, such as artwork, placing importance on their ability to be creative. Tommy's fascination with his own creativity is evidence of the importance artwork plays in the students' own personal identities. Later, Tommy and Kathy both think that their artwork will help them secure a deferral.

Being a student of Hailsham itself allows a certain sense of identity. Kathy speaks of being from Hailsham with fondness and pride. She often mentions how other students view Hailsham students with envy. Throughout the text, Kathy describes a number of rumours of privileges supposedly allowed to former Hailsham students.

As they grow older, many characters express a desire to find out where they came from. For Kathy, this is shown by her fascination with pornographic magazines. For Ruth, and many others, it is finding their possible. Both Kathy and Ruth feel that they're cloned from the less desirable elements of society.

How does the 'outside world' view the students?

In Part Three, Miss Emily and Madame provide the most information regarding how society views the students. Prior to this, the reader is only given small bits of information through Miss Lucy or Kathy's own musings on the outside world.

In general, people view the students with disgust. They do not see them as human; they are medical by-products. Instead, they prefer for them to be 'out of sight, out of mind'.

A small group of people, Miss Emily and Madame included, were part of a campaign for better living conditions for the clones. This included the creation of schools such as Hailsham.

Key Quotations to Learn

... how much you were liked and respected, had to do with how good you were at 'creating'. (Kathy: Chapter 2)

'*Art* students, that's what she thought we were. Do you think she'd have talked to us like that if she'd known what we really were?' (Ruth: Chapter 14)

'As you say, why would anyone doubt you had a soul? But I have to tell you, my dear, it wasn't something commonly held when we first set out all those years ago.' (Miss Emily: Chapter 22)

Summary

- Students create their own identities through keeping small trinkets in their collections.
- Creativity is valued as part of their personal identity.
- Most students go through a period of curiosity about where they came from.
- The outside world largely views the students as expendable.

Sample Analysis

The students' curiosity about their identity can be seen when Kathy describes looking at pornography magazines. She describes how she 'moved through the pages quickly, not wanting to be distracted by the buzz of sex' and that she 'hardly saw the contorted bodies, because [she] was focusing on the faces'. The use of the adverbs 'quickly' and 'hardly' show that she was not looking at the pictures for personal pleasure. This is further emphasised through the use of verbs such as 'moved' and 'focusing on the faces', which shows a detached, clinical view of the pornography. We later learn that she was trying to find her possible amongst the faces in the magazines.

Questions

QUICK TEST
1. How do the students create their own sense of identity whilst at Hailsham?
2. Why do the students value skills such as creativity?
3. Why are the students interested in finding their possibles?
4. How do most people view the students?
5. What makes Madame and Miss Emily different, in terms of their views of the students?

EXAM PRACTICE
Using one or more of the 'Key Quotations to Learn', write about how Ishiguro presents the theme of identity in the text.

Nostalgia

You must be able to: analyse how the theme of nostalgia is presented in the text.

What is nostalgia?

Nostalgia is a sentimental desire to return to, or look back upon, a previous part of your life. Often this includes feelings of happiness about an earlier time or place.

Why is Kathy nostalgic?

Most of the novel centres around Kathy remembering different parts of her life: Hailsham, the Cottages and her final days with Ruth and Tommy. Due to her job as carer, which she describes as very solitary, she spends much of her time driving from one recovery centre to another. During her time alone, she reminisces about her life.

By the end of the novel, Kathy appears to have lost everything. Ruth and Tommy are gone, having completed their donations; Hailsham is lost to her, both because she doesn't know where to find it and because it was closed; and the people she knew from the Cottages have largely exited her life as well.

Kathy places a lot of importance on her memories and expresses frustration when other former Hailsham students appear to forget their past.

Why aren't other characters as nostalgic as Kathy?

Ishiguro makes it clear that Hailsham was a 'special' place at various points throughout the text. Kathy often describes how her donors never wanted to talk about their own past; instead, they ask her to describe Hailsham.

Similarly, Chrissie and Rodney do not talk much about their past, instead focusing on what it was like at Hailsham. This is likely because they were at more brutal centres described by Miss Emily: the reader is given the impression that these places are inhumane and unhappy.

However, other Hailsham characters, such as Ruth or Tommy, do not express as much sentiment as Kathy. Ruth throws her collection away at the Cottages and fails to remember things that Kathy does.

Key Quotations to Learn

... I asked where *he'd* grown up, he mentioned some place in Dorset and his face beneath the blotches went into a completely new kind of grimace. And I realise how desperately he didn't want to be reminded. (Kathy: Chapter 1)

Driving around the country now, I still see things that remind me of Hailsham. (Kathy: Chapter 1)

I lost Ruth, then I lost Tommy, but I won't lose my memories of them. (Kathy: Chapter 23)

Summary

- Kathy looks back on her past with fondness.
- Many of her memories are tied to Hailsham.
- Other characters, especially those from outside Hailsham, are less inclined to remember things.

Sample Analysis

Kathy looks back on her past with fondness. For example, in Chapter 18 she uses a simile comparing Hailsham to a bunch of helium balloons. When she hears about Hailsham closing, she says that 'it was like someone coming along with a pair of shears and snipping the balloon strings'. This troubles her, because 'there'd be no real sense in which those balloons belonged with each other any more'. The balloons in this simile represent herself and the other Hailsham students, such as Ruth and Tommy. With Hailsham closing, she feels as though they no longer have anything tying them together. It is after she makes this **analogy** that she decides to become Ruth's carer.

Questions

QUICK TEST
1. Why does Kathy spend so much time remembering the past?
2. Why do other students like to talk so much about Hailsham, but not their own pasts?
3. How does Kathy feel when other students claim to forget things she remembers?

EXAM PRACTICE
Using one or more of the 'Key Quotations to Learn', write about how Ishiguro presents the theme of nostalgia in the text.

You must be able to: analyse how the theme of friendship is presented in the text.

What is friendship?

Friendship is a relationship of trust and respect between people. It is stronger than merely being an acquaintance, but lacks the physical element of romantic love. Friends typically care for each other, providing support to one another.

How is friendship in the novel different to our own understanding of friendship?

The students at Hailsham act very much like 'normal' children, teenagers, and later, young adults. They go through the same developmental stages, such as making and losing friends and vying for affection and attention from others.

However, the difference is that the students can only interact with each other. They are not able to form friendships with adults or anyone from outside of their small community.

How is friendship presented throughout the text?

Ishiguro presents a realistic version of teenage friendship through the relationship between Ruth and Kathy. Ruth is shown to be very bossy and dominant. She controls much of the behaviour of other girls, especially while at Hailsham, and Kathy is often swept along with this. There are many instances in the text where Kathy does things to gain Ruth's approval.

However, their friendship is tumultuous. Kathy often becomes tired of Ruth's lies and tries to catch her out a few times. For example, she reveals how Ruth lied about receiving a pencil case from Miss Geraldine and points out that her behaviour at the Cottages is ridiculous. Later, Kathy shows regret for pointing out Ruth's lies/behaviour.

Ruth is not the perfect friend either: she later admits to keeping Tommy and Kathy apart, and often ignores or insults Kathy at the Cottages. It is Ruth's humiliation of Kathy that causes Kathy to leave the Cottages.

The strength of their friendship is evident at the end of the novel, when Kathy becomes Ruth's carer. They quickly re-establish their previous relationship. Ruth tries to right the wrongs of the past by bringing Kathy and Tommy together and providing them with Madame's address.

Key Quotations to Learn

I was never sure if Ruth had actually invented the secret guard herself, but there was no doubt she was the leader. (Kathy: Chapter 5)

We didn't do things like hug each other much at Hailsham. But I squeezed one of her hands in both of mine when I thanked her. (Kathy: Chapter 6)

It's an object, like a brooch or a ring, and especially now that Ruth has gone, it's become one of my most precious possessions. (Kathy: Chapter 6)

Summary

- Friendship with each other is one of the only forms of social contact the students are encouraged to have.
- Ruth and Kathy have a realistic female relationship.
- Kathy values her friendships with Ruth and Tommy highly.

Sample Analysis

Kathy has a complicated relationship with Ruth. For example, despite being excluded by Ruth from the secret guard, she continues to work for her approval. When Moira insults Ruth, Kathy is 'puzzled by the sheer force of the emotion that overtook' her in defending Ruth. She no longer felt 'angry' at Ruth for excluding her, and instead was 'just hugely irritated with Moira'. The verb 'puzzled' emphasises Kathy's confusion; she was initially 'angry' at Ruth, but overall her feelings of loyalty outweighed her anger. The fact that Kathy 'wasn't prepared' to 'cross that line' against Ruth shows how complex their relationship was.

Questions

QUICK TEST
1. How are the students' friendships with each other the same as modern teen friendships?
2. What aspects of Ruth and Kathy's relationship seem realistic?
3. Why does Ruth provide Kathy and Tommy with Madame's address?

EXAM PRACTICE
Using one or more of the 'Key Quotations to Learn', write about how Ishiguro presents the theme of friendship in the text.

You must be able to: analyse how the theme of love is presented in the text.

What is love?

Love can be used to describe strong emotions towards something or someone. There are a lot of different types of love, but typically love refers to intense, often intimate, feelings of admiration and attraction. Love can be familial, as the love between a mother and daughter, or romantic and physical, as the love between two unrelated people. Friendships can also be loving.

How does Ishiguro present love in the text?

Through the relationships between the students, Ishiguro shows the reader how powerful love can be. He presents many different sides of love throughout the text, including young love, loving friendship and even loving companionship. By doing so, he suggests that love is an emotion that makes us truly human.

The loving relationship between Kathy and Tommy is developed throughout the text. It is clear from the beginning that their friendship could one day develop into romantic love. Other characters even hint at this when Ruth and Tommy first break up at Hailsham. However, Ruth's jealously keeps them apart.

When Tommy and Kathy finally become a couple, their relationship is tinged with sadness due to the fact that they left it so late. They have very little time together as a couple, which is tragic.

Ruth believes that Tommy and Kathy are truly in love. She feels regret for keeping them apart in the past and provides them with Madame's address because she thinks they have a chance of getting a deferral.

The fact that the students think love will save them from their duty to be carers and donors, even if just for a short time, emphasises Ishiguro's belief in the power of love. Through the students, he shows us the redemptive quality of love and the importance people place on love in society.

However, he also highlights the complexity of love. When the students turn up to see Madame, claiming that they're in love, she questions them about how they can be certain of this. Tommy thinks his artwork will prove his love, but Madame's reaction shows how absurd this concept is. Being in love is not something that can necessarily be proven.

Ultimately, it is Kathy's love for Ruth and Tommy that makes the ending of the story so poignant. She is left alone, with nothing but memories of the people and places that she once loved.

Key Quotations to Learn

... I'd been Tommy's friend for years until all this couples stuff [...] It was perfectly possible that to someone on the outside, I'd look like Ruth's 'natural successor'. (Kathy: Chapter 9)

I'm sure Tommy felt it too, because we'd always hold each other very tight after times like that, as though that way we'd manage to keep the feeling away. (Kathy: Chapter 20)

'Tommy and me, we would never have come and bothered you if we weren't really sure.' (Kathy: Chapter 21)

Summary

- Kathy's love of Hailsham, Tommy and Ruth runs throughout the text.
- The love between Kathy and Tommy is tragic.
- Love is presented as an experience that makes us human.

Sample Analysis

The last time Kathy sees Tommy highlights their love for each other. Tommy, not wanting Kathy to see him suffer, asks her to find a new donor. As she leaves, she describes how 'we kissed – just a small kiss' and that she 'watched him in [her] rear-view mirror, and he was standing there almost till the last moment'. The adjective 'small' shows a delicacy to their relationship, while the fact that Tommy watched 'almost till the last moment' emphasises a reluctance to let go. The tone set in this scene is one of sadness and heartbreak; neither character wants to part.

Questions

QUICK TEST
1. Why does Ruth keep Tommy and Kathy apart?
2. What do the students think they need in order to get a deferral?
3. What does Madame say when Tommy and Kathy claim to be in love?

EXAM PRACTICE
Using one or more of the 'Key Quotations to Learn', write about how Ishiguro presents the theme of love in the text.

Hopes and Dreams/the Future

You must be able to: analyse how the theme of hopes and dreams is presented in the text.

What is meant by hopes and dreams?

To have hope means to want, look forward to, or expect something in the future. Similarly, having dreams refers to hopeful imaginings for the future, often in an indulgent sense.

What hopes and dreams do the students have for themselves?

Even though the students are aware of the purpose of their lives, and the fact that they will not live long, they still have hopes and dreams for themselves.

Throughout the novel, it is clear that Kathy hopes to be with Tommy. However, every time there is a chance of them getting together, something seems to keep them apart; this is often Ruth, but ultimately it is their own fate. Nevertheless, Kathy remains hopeful until the very end; the text ends with Kathy daydreaming about finding her childhood, and ultimately Tommy, while standing near a field in Norfolk.

At Hailsham, Kathy describes students discussing what it might be like to work in certain jobs and travel the world. However, when Miss Lucy hears this kind of talk, she quickly puts an end to it, because she thinks such dreaming is harmful.

Ruth is described as having a dream of working in an office. That's why, when Rodney suggests her possible might be in an office in Cromer, she is quite eager to see for herself. Her angry reaction after seeing her possible emphasises her disappointment, as her dream has been shattered.

Tommy later describes Ruth as a dreamer. He suggests that of all the characters, she was the one who held the most hope for the future.

Tommy places a lot of hope in his artwork – he continues to create drawings because he thinks that they might help him get a deferral. He is disillusioned when he finds out that deferrals are nothing but a rumour.

When asked why they allow this rumour to continue, Miss Emily suggests that it was too hard to take away that hope. Whenever she tried to kill the rumour, it would always pop up again.

Chrissie – as well as some of Kathy's donors – dreams of what it might have been like to be a Hailsham student. They are fascinated by the students of Hailsham and wonder what it would have been like had they lived there themselves. They place their hopes in Hailsham students, trying to get insider information and prestige. Hailsham students give others hope that there is a better life available.

Key Quotations to Learn

'None of you will go to America, none of you will be film stars. And none of you will be working in supermarkets as I heard some of you planning the other day.' (Miss Lucy: Chapter 7)

'You and Tommy, you've got to try and get a deferral. If it's you two, there's got to be a chance. A real chance.' (Ruth: Chapter 19)

'It's something for them to dream about, a little fantasy. What harm is there?' (Miss Emily: Chapter 22)

Summary

- The students dream of living full lives, despite knowing this will never happen.
- Kathy and Tommy place their hopes in the deferral rumour and are disappointed when it turns out to be untrue.
- The novel ends with Kathy daydreaming about Tommy, finding all the things she has lost.

Sample Analysis

Kathy and Tommy describe Ruth as a believer. They are happy that she completed before finding out that deferrals were not real. Kathy says that if Ruth had learned the truth 'it would have made her feel bad; made her see the damage she'd once done to us couldn't be repaired as easily as she'd hoped'. Kathy expresses a small comfort in knowing that Ruth would never 'feel bad' and 'see the damage' she had done. These verb phrases are effective because they allow the reader to sympathise with Ruth; she was able to die with hope for Kathy and Tommy's future.

Questions

QUICK TEST
1. Why does Miss Lucy stop the students from talking about their future?
2. Why is Ruth so disappointed when the woman in Cromer looks nothing like her?
3. Why does Miss Emily allow the deferral rumour to continue?
4. Why do students from outside Hailsham look up to Hailsham students?

EXAM PRACTICE
Using one or more of the 'Key Quotations to Learn', write about how Ishiguro presents the theme of hopes and dreams in the text.

Freedom

You must be able to: analyse how Ishiguro presents the theme of freedom across the text.

What is freedom?

Freedom is the state of being free or at liberty, rather than in confinement or under physical restraint. To be free means that you are not under the power or control of someone or something else; you can make choices for yourself.

How free are the students of Hailsham?

Kathy often refers to the fences and the forest around Hailsham. Generally, there is a feeling of fear of what lies outside the school. Students create scary stories about going into the woods, which effectively keep them from venturing too far.

Miss Lucy casually mentions how fences around other **rearing** facilities are electrified, stating that the fences around Hailsham are not.

The students of Hailsham rarely interact with people from outside of the school. Their ability to socialise is therefore highly controlled and regulated.

How free are the students while at the Cottages?

At the Cottages, students have more freedom than at Hailsham. They can take day trips out and are taught how to drive. However, they must sign in and out, suggesting that they are expected to return.

The students also experience some social freedom while at the Cottages. They can interact with students from outside Hailsham and from the outside world. However, their contact with 'normal' people is limited – there are barriers here too, which the students themselves acknowledge.

How free are the students when acting as carers and donors?

Again, there is relative freedom during this stage of their lives; however, there is always an element of control and obligation. Kathy describes driving all over the country, but these trips are for her work as a carer. When she takes Ruth and Tommy to see the abandoned boat and when they go to see Madame, they return in one day.

Social freedom is limited. Kathy interacts with nurses and doctors, but there is very little interaction with anyone outside of this medical circle. Most of her social contact is with other clones.

What does Miss Emily think of the clones' freedom?

Miss Emily suggests that they had freedoms that were not afforded to other clones. She suggests that, intellectually, they were free to develop thoughts and feelings. However, she acknowledges that they will never have true freedom.

Key Quotations to Learn

'It's just as well the fences at Hailsham aren't electrified. You get terrible accidents sometimes.' (Miss Lucy: Chapter 7)

'We all knew no one would stop us if we wandered off, provided we were back by the day and the time we entered into Keffers's ledgerbook.' (Kathy: Chapter 10)

... I do like the feeling of getting into my little car, knowing that for the next couple of hours I'll have only the roads, the big grey sky and my daydreams for company. (Kathy: Chapter 18)

Summary

- Hailsham students have more freedom than clones in other centres, but they are kept separate from the outside world.
- The students gain relative freedom at the Cottages and when caring/donating, but they are still separated from wider society.
- Ultimately, freedom is denied to the clones – they will always be expected to care and donate their body parts.

Sample Analysis

Kathy describes how the students used to dream of growing up and the freedom that would come with it. She says that they would take 'comfort' in the idea that 'when we were grown up' and 'were free to travel around the country' they could track down things that were 'precious' to them. The verbs 'comfort' and 'free to travel' show her positive hopes for the future. Interestingly, these also show a very stereotypical view children have of the future – that grown-up life will be much more free and enjoyable. The reality, for clones and 'normal' people alike, is often less rosy than that.

Questions

QUICK TEST
1. How are the fences at Hailsham different from other rearing facilities?
2. What must the students do whenever they leave the Cottages?
3. Why does Kathy drive all over England?

EXAM PRACTICE
Using one or more of the 'Key Quotations to Learn', write about how Ishiguro presents the theme of freedom in the text.

Humanity

You must be able to: analyse how Ishiguro presents the theme of humanity across the text.

What is humanity?

Humanity refers to the condition and qualities of being human.

What makes us human?

There is not a straightforward answer to this question, and this is something Ishiguro highlights throughout the novel. Scientifically, humans are derived from *Homo sapiens*. Being human refers to having certain characteristics that define us as human. These include standing upright, using tools, having intelligent thought, living in social communities and having shared language.

How does Ishiguro problematise humanity in the text?

Using the definition above, the students in the novel would be classed as human beings. Kathy describes her childhood, teenage years and mid-twenties in a way that seems very relatable to **contemporary** readers. The problems she faces are typical of many young people.

However, Ishiguro presents a world in which Kathy and her friends are not viewed as normal youths. Instead, they are bio-medically cloned beings, produced for the sole purpose of providing tissue and organs to other human beings. As such, it is more convenient for society to view them as sub-human; not to do so would raise too many human rights and **ethical** issues. To see the clones as human would mean an end to the cloning programme.

The students therefore spend their lives on the fringes of society; they grow up in various facilities across the country, spend some time living in small communities outside of these initial care facilities and then move on to donating and, ultimately, death.

Miss Emily and Madame are presented as people in society who are against this type of treatment of clones. They created Hailsham to show the rest of the world that clones are capable of thought, reasoning and artistic skill, all of which highlight their humanity. However, it is unclear if they were campaigning for an end to cloning or just for better treatment of clones.

However, Miss Emily also admits that her idealistic view of better treatment for clones could not succeed if the donation programme was to continue. It is suggested that society is too reliant on the benefits provided by cloning: people would rather turn a blind eye to the ethical issues so that they can continue to benefit from cloning.

Hailsham is therefore a social experiment. Through Miss Emily and Madame's veiled comments, and through Kathy's own vague conversations with others, the reader is presented with an appalling system of neglect and poor hygiene in other clone facilities.

Ultimately though, death is something that all humans must face. The difference in this novel is that the students do not get to live normal, full lives, nor do they get to choose the type of lives they lead.

Key Quotations to Learn

'But what you must understand is that for you, for all of you, it's much, much worse to smoke than it ever was for me.' (Miss Lucy: Chapter 6)

... people out there were different from us students: they could have babies from sex. (Kathy: Chapter 7)

'We took away your art because we thought it would reveal your souls. Or to put it more finely, we did it *to prove you had souls at all.*' (Miss Emily: Chapter 22)

Summary

- Ishiguro presents a complicated view of what makes us human.
- The students view themselves as human: they are shocked at the notion of not knowing love or not having souls.
- The rest of the world does not want to view clones as human.

Sample Analysis

Miss Emily describes how 'there are students being reared in deplorable conditions'. The use of the verb 'reared' suggests a sense of detachment from the students; the word 'reared' is often used to describe the raising of animals. Similarly, she uses the adjective 'deplorable' to describe their conditions, which again suggests they live in an inhumane environment. Overall, this quote shows how differently the clones are treated compared with the rest of society.

Questions

QUICK TEST
1. How does Ishiguro present Kathy and her friends as typical young people?
2. Why were the clones created?
3. Why did Miss Emily and Madame establish Hailsham?
4. Why does the Hailsham project fail?

EXAM PRACTICE
Using one or more of the 'Key Quotations to Learn', write about how Ishiguro presents the theme of humanity in the text.

Lies and Deceit

You must be able to: analyse how Ishiguro presents the theme of lies and deceit across the text.

What does it mean to deceive or lie?

To deceive someone is to mislead them by giving them false information or through a false appearance. Similarly, a lie is an intentionally false statement told to deceive or mislead someone.

Which characters are seen to deceive or lie to others?

The guardians at Hailsham continually deceive the children by not telling them the full truth about their existence. According to Miss Emily, this was done to ensure they lived happy lives and as a form of protection. However, Miss Lucy takes issue with this viewpoint and attempts to tell them the truth; she is fired for doing so.

Ruth is seen to lie frequently. For example, she pretends to be a chess expert and lies about receiving her pencil case from Miss Geraldine. The extent of her lying is well known by the other students; Moira says 'It's just another of Ruth's made-up things'.

Kathy herself can sometimes be deceptive. She casually confronts Ruth about the truth of the pencil case and she pretends to be happy when she receives an unwanted tape from Ruth.

Ruth deceives Kathy often whilst at the Cottages. For example, she tells her that her 'urges' are not normal and, worst of all, she tells Kathy that Tommy will never see her in a romantic way. She betrays Kathy's trust by telling Tommy things that Kathy said to her in private. Ruth does this out of jealousy.

Not all of Ruth's lies stem from jealousy though. She misleads Chrissy and Rodney about the perks of being a Hailsham student to fit in.

Kathy also deceives herself, throughout the text, by not admitting her feelings for Tommy until it is too late. She also does not admit freely to the reasons behind her study of the pornographic magazines. Similarly, she does not express her doubts about Tommy's artwork and deferrals to Tommy.

The biggest deception comes from Miss Emily; the purpose of Hailsham itself, coupled with Madame's Gallery, was hidden from the students. She never told the children the truth about their lives because she felt it was better for them to be blissfully ignorant. She also allowed the deferral rumour to continue, despite knowing that it was nothing more than a misguided dream.

Which characters see themselves as honest?

Both Kathy and Miss Emily think that they are open and honest.

Kathy, in her narration, refers to the fact that she might not remember things exactly as they took place, but that does not stop her from sharing her interpretation; this makes her narration slightly unreliable and biased.

Miss Emily is steadfast in her determination that she did the right thing at Hailsham. She deliberately misled the students about their futures, but in her mind, it was for a good reason. She feels nothing but pride for her role and offers no apologies for what she has done in the past.

Key Quotations to Learn

This was all a long time ago so I might have some of it wrong. (Kathy: Chapter 2)

It was always stuff like that, and never explicitly claimed, just implied by her smile and 'let's say no more' expression. (Kathy: Chapter 5)

'If you're going to have decent lives, you have to know who you are and what lies ahead of you, every one of you.' (Miss Lucy: Chapter 7)

Summary

- Much like normal people, the students lie to each other for their own personal gain.
- Miss Lucy was the only honest character.
- Miss Emily felt as though her deception was necessary and right.

Sample Analysis

Miss Emily feels justified in lying to the students. She says that 'we sheltered you during those years, and we gave you your childhoods'. The use of a **compound sentence** here shows that she feels the two things, lying and providing a good childhood, are connected and that the good outweighs the bad. Similarly, she uses the verb 'sheltered' instead of 'lied' to put a more positive **connotation** on what she did.

Questions

QUICK TEST
1. Why do the guardians at Hailsham lie to the students?
2. Why is Miss Lucy fired?
3. What sort of things does Ruth lie about?
4. How is Kathy shown to deceive herself?

EXAM PRACTICE
Using one or more of the 'Key Quotations to Learn', write about how Ishiguro presents the theme of lies/deception in the text.

Tips and Assessment Objectives

You must be able to: understand how to approach the exam question and meet the requirements of the mark scheme.

Quick tips

- You will get a choice of two questions. Do the one that best matches your knowledge, the quotations you have learned and the things you have revised.

- Make sure you know what the question is asking you. Underline key words and pay particular attention to the bullet point prompts that come with the question.

- You should spend about 45 minutes on your *Never Let Me Go* response. Allow yourself five minutes to plan your answer so there is some structure to your essay.

- All your paragraphs should contain a clear idea, a relevant reference to the text (ideally a quotation) and analysis of how Ishiguro conveys the idea. Whenever possible, you should link your comments to the novel's context.

- It can sometimes help, after each paragraph, to quickly re-read the question to keep yourself focussed on the exam task.

- Keep your writing concise. If you waste time 'waffling' you won't be able to include the full range of analysis and understand what the mark scheme requires.

- It is a good idea to remember what the mark scheme is asking of you.

AO1: Understand and respond to the novel (12 marks)

This is all about coming up with a range of points that match the question, supporting your ideas with references from the novel and writing your essay in a mature, academic style.

Lower	Middle	Upper
The essay has some good ideas that are mostly relevant. Some quotations and references are used to support the ideas.	A clear essay that always focuses on the exam question. Quotations and references support ideas effectively. The response refers to different points of the text.	A convincing, well-structured essay that answers the question fully. Quotations and references are well-chosen and integrated into sentences. The response covers the whole text (not everything, but ideas from across the text rather than just focussing on one or two sections).

AO2: Analysing effects of Ishiguro's language, form and structure (12 marks)

You need to comment on how specific words, language techniques, sentence structures, dialogue or the narrative structure allow Ishiguro to get his ideas across to the reader. This could simply be something about a character or a larger idea he is exploring through the text. To achieve this, you will need to have learned good quotations to analyse.

Lower	Middle	Upper
Identification of some different methods used by Ishiguro to convey meaning. Some subject terminology.	Explanation of Ishiguro's different methods. Clear understanding of the effects of these methods. Accurate use of subject terminology.	Analysis of the full range of Ishiguro's methods. Thorough exploration of the effects of these methods. Accurate range of subject terminology.

AO3: Understand the relationship between the novel and its contexts (6 marks)

For this part of the mark scheme, you need to show your understanding of how the characters or Ishiguro's ideas relate to when he was writing (early 2000s) or when the novel was set (1990s/early 2000s).

Lower	Middle	Upper
Some awareness of how ideas in the novel link to its context.	References to relevant aspects of context show a clear understanding.	Exploration is linked to specific aspects of the novel's contexts to show a detailed understanding.

AO4: Written accuracy (4 marks)

You need to use accurate vocabulary, expression, punctuation and spelling. Although it's only four marks, this could make the difference between a lower or higher grade.

Lower	Middle	Upper
Reasonable level of accuracy. Errors do not get in the way of the essay making sense.	Good level of accuracy. Vocabulary and sentences help to keep ideas clear.	Consistent high level of accuracy. Vocabulary and sentences are used to make ideas clear and precise.

1. What do you think is the importance of the ending of *Never Let Me Go*?

   Write about:
   - how the end of the text presents some important ideas
   - how Ishiguro presents these ideas by the way he writes the text.

2. How does Ishiguro use the character of Kathy to explore ideas of humanity in *Never Let Me Go*?

   Write about:
   - how Ishiguro presents Kathy
   - how Ishiguro uses Kathy to explore some of his ideas about being human.

3. How does Ishiguro present the relationship between Kathy and Ruth throughout *Never Let Me Go*?

   Write about:
   - what their relationship is like
   - how Ishiguro uses the relationship to present some of his ideas.

4. 'Ruth is presented as a manipulative character in *Never Let Me Go*'. Explore how far you agree with this statement.

   Write about:
   - how Ishiguro presents the character of Ruth
   - how Ishiguro uses Ruth to explore some of his ideas.

5. Which character shows the most hope for the future in *Never Let Me Go*?

   Write about:
   - how Ishiguro presents your chosen character
   - how Ishiguro uses your chosen character to explore some of his ideas.

6. How is Tommy presented as a figure of sympathy in *Never Let Me Go*?

   Write about:
   - the way Tommy speaks and behaves
   - how Ishiguro presents Tommy in the text.

7. 'In *Never Let Me Go* Kathy is a kind, caring figure'. Explore how far you agree with this statement.

   Write about:
   - how Ishiguro presents the character of Kathy
   - how Ishiguro uses the character of Kathy to explore some of his ideas.

8. In *Never Let Me Go*, Madame says 'You say you're sure? Sure that you're in love? How can you know it?' How does Ishiguro explore issues about love?

   Write about:
   - how Ishiguro presents issues about love
   - how Ishiguro uses these views to explore ideas about humanity.

9. Kathy says that 'I've told myself I shouldn't look back so much. But then there came a point when I just stopped resisting'. How does Ishiguro explore nostalgia in the text?

   Write about:

   - how Ishiguro presents Kathy's memories of the past
   - how Ishiguro uses these memories to explore issues around nostalgia.

10. How does Ishiguro present the relationship between Kathy and Tommy throughout *Never Let Me Go*?

    Write about:

    - what their relationship is like
    - how Ishiguro uses their relationship to present some of his ideas.

11. Kathy describes how people were 'fascinated – obsessed in some cases' with finding their possible.

    How does Ishiguro present ideas about identity in the text?

    Write about:

    - what some of the ideas about identity are
    - how Ishiguro presents ideas of identity throughout the text.

12. Do Kathy and Ruth have a good friendship?

    Write about:

    - how Ishiguro presents the friendship between Kathy and Ruth
    - how Ishiguro uses Kathy and Ruth to explore ideas about friendship.

13. How does Ishiguro use Hailsham to explore ideas about hope and dreams for the future in *Never Let Me Go*?

    Write about:

    - how Ishiguro presents ideas about hope and dreams for the future
    - how Ishiguro uses Hailsham to explore some of his ideas.

14. Miss Lucy says 'If you're to have decent lives, you have to know who you are and what lies ahead of you, every one of you'. She feels that the students are not told enough about the reality of their lives.

    To what extent do you agree with her views?

    Write about:

    - how Ishiguro presents Miss Lucy's views about the students
    - how Ishiguro uses Miss Lucy's views to explore some of his ideas about humanity.

15. 'Miss Emily did the right thing by allowing the rumour of deferrals to exist'. Explore how far you agree with this statement.

    Write about:

    - how Ishiguro presents the character of Miss Emily
    - how Ishiguro uses Miss Emily to explore some of his ideas.

Planning a Character Question Response

You must be able to: understand what an exam question is asking you and prepare your response.

How might an exam question be phrased?

A typical character question will read like this:

How and why does Ruth change in *Never Let Me Go*? Write about:

- how Ruth talks and behaves towards others
- how Ishiguro presents Ruth by the way he writes.

[30 marks + 4 AO4 marks]

How do I work out what to do?

The focus of the question is clear: Ruth and how her character changes.

'How' and 'why' are important elements of this question.

For AO1, these words show that you need to display a clear understanding of what Ruth is like, the ways in which she changes and the reasons for these changes.

For AO2, 'how' makes it clear that you need to analyse the different ways in which Ishiguro's use of language, structure and form help to show the reader what Ruth is like. Ideally, you should include quotations that you have learnt but, if necessary, you can make clear references to a specific part of the text.

You also need to remember to link your comments to the novel's context to achieve your AO3 marks and write accurately to pick up your four AO4 marks for spelling, punctuation and grammar.

How can I plan my essay?

You have approximately 45 minutes to write your essay.

This isn't long, but you should spend the first five minutes writing a quick plan. This will help you to focus your response and produce a well-structured essay.

Try to come up with five or six ideas. Each of these ideas can then be written up as a paragraph.

You can plan in whatever way you find most useful. Some students like to make a quick list of points and then re-number them into a logical order. Others like to use spider diagrams; look at the example on the opposite page.

At the start of the text, Ruth is shown to be manipulative and controlling. The other students, including Kathy, look to her for direction.

'I was never sure if Ruth had actually invented the secret guard herself, but there was no doubt she was the leader.'
(Kathy: Chapter 5)

Lies about herself in order to make herself look special.

'"Let's just agree. Let's *agree* I got it in the Sale." Then she gave us all a knowing smile.'
(Ruth to Kathy: Chapter 5)
(Context: growing up – self-identity)

How and why Ruth changes

Jealous of Kathy's relationship with Tommy, Ruth tries to keep them apart.

'Tommy and I were made for each other and he'll listen to you. You'll do this for us, won't you Kathy?'
(Ruth: Chapter 9)

She is rude and dismissive to Kathy and Tommy at the Cottages because she is desperate to fit in.

'Oh, look who's upset now. Poor Kathy. She never likes straight talking.'
(Ruth: Chapter 14)
(Context: friendship and identity)

She is mean and resentful of being left out by Kathy and Tommy.

'Tommy's telling me about his big theory. He says he's already told you. Ages ago. But now, very kindly, he's allowing me to share in it too.'
(Ruth: Chapter 15)

At the end of the text, Ruth has changed. She admits that she lied to Kathy in the past. She brings Kathy and Tommy together and gives them Madame's address because she wants to make up for her past mistakes.

'Forgive me for what? Well, for starters, there's the way I always lied to you about your urges.'

'The main thing is, I kept you and Tommy apart.'
(Ruth: Chapter 19)

(Context: growing up – maturity that comes with age)

 Questions

QUICK TEST
1. What key skills do you need to show in your answer?
2. What are the benefits of quickly planning your essay?
3. Why is it better to have learned quotations for the exam?

EXAM PRACTICE

Plan a response to the following exam question:

How and why does Tommy change in *Never Let Me Go*? Write about:
- how Tommy talks and behaves towards others
- how Ishiguro presents Tommy by the way he writes.

[30 marks + 4 AO4 marks]

Grade 5 Annotated Response

How and why does Ruth change in *Never Let Me Go*? Write about:
- how Ruth talks and behaves towards others
- how Ishiguro presents Ruth by the way he writes.

[30 marks + 4 AO4 marks]

In Part One of the text Ruth is presented as popular and well liked. She clearly enjoys being in control and acts much like a confident young girl would. For example, it is Ruth who sets up the secret guard for Miss Geraldine, as well as the trap for Madame (1). When other girls start to question her, she excludes them from the group. For example, Kathy says that 'if she decided that someone should be expelled' then they were out of the group. The tone used here, with verbs like 'decided' and 'expelled' show how in control she was (2). Even Kathy suffers from this treatment when she begins to question where Ruth got the pencil case from. But when Ruth reacts with embarrassment, Kathy quickly finds herself on Ruth's bad side and has to work hard to win back her friendship (3).

Ruth also manipulated Kathy's relationship with Tommy because she was jealous of them (4). When Ruth and Tommy break up, other students suggest that Kathy would be a natural successor to her. However, Ruth does not like this, and so she goes to Kathy and makes her convince Tommy to take her back. 'Tommy and I are made for each other' (5). Ruth uses a **simple sentence** here to make it sound like fact, giving Kathy no choice but to help.

In Part Two, at the Cottages, Ruth continues to act this way. However, here she is shown as more insecure, reflecting the fact that she is now a teenager (6). She looks to the veterans for guidance, and is eager to please them and fit in. Kathy says that Ruth was 'putting on airs and pretending'. She talks about there being 'two quite separate Ruths', which is different from Hailsham, because she is no longer in control. However, she tries to maintain some of her former power by continuing to manipulate Kathy and Tommy. She maintains a friendship with Kathy, confiding in her, but is quick to use what Kathy says against her to gain her own social mobility and to keep Kathy and Tommy apart. For example, she tells Tommy 'Kathy here finds your animals a complete hoot'. This simple sentence was hurtful to Tommy and broke her trust with Kathy.

It isn't until Ruth leaves the Cottages and becomes a donor in Part Three that she really changes. Some time away from the others, as well as going through a tough donation, provides her with some perspective. Going through this painful procedure alone has matured her, making her realise how poorly she treated her friends in the past (7). When Kathy turns up to become her carer, it is clear Ruth struggles to come to terms with her past behaviour. Kathy sees this as tension between them. She describes how 'the sense of something not being right grew stronger and stronger' and how their conversations became 'more stilted and guarded'. These adjectives show that Ruth finds it hard to speak to Kathy because of their past.

When Ruth opens up to Kathy and Tommy we finally see how much she has changed. She admits that she 'lied' to Kathy before and that she 'kept' Kathy and Tommy apart (8). She even says that she 'can't see' why Kathy should forgive her herself. It is clear that Ruth has grown and matured a lot since the start of the text and she knows what she did was wrong, but she tries to fix her mistakes by getting Tommy and Kathy Madame's address, so they can have 'a real chance' at a deferral (9). Again, this simple sentence suggests that it is fact, encouraging Kathy and Tommy to take the opportunity she has presented them with (10).

1. The first paragraph has a clear idea and is supported by references to the novel. AO1
2. Clear analysis of the effects of Ishiguro's language choices. Some terminology is used. AO2
3. There is some explanation of the methods Ishiguro uses to show Ruth's character. This is limited by the lack of quotations. AO1/AO2
4. This new paragraph introduces a new point and is focussed on the question of how and why Ruth changes. AO1
5. A relevant quotation is used here. It would be better if it were embedded in a sentence. AO1
6. Some social context is used to explain Ruth's behaviour but it is a little generalised. AO3
7. Social context is used to develop the explanation. AO3
8. A quotation is embedded effectively but it isn't analysed. AO1/AO2
9. The writing could be more careful and mature as this sentence is quite long and the vocabulary is simple. However, the link back to the start of the text is an effective way of responding to the question. AO1
10. Overall, the final paragraph offers some conclusion, but it is a little rushed. The essay could be structured more effectively, as several ideas are included all at once. Writing is clear and accurate but doesn't enhance the essay. AO1/AO4

Questions

EXAM PRACTICE
Choose a paragraph of this essay. Read it through a few times, then try to rewrite and improve it. You might:
*   Improve the sophistication of the language or the clarity of expression.
*   Replace the references to the text with quotations or use better quotations.
*   Ensure quotations are embedded in the sentence.
*   Provide more detailed, or a wider range of, analysis.
*   Use more subject terminology.
*   Link some context to the analysis more effectively.

Grade 7+ Annotated Response

> A proportion of the best top-band answers will be awarded Grade 8 or Grade 9. To achieve this, you should aim for a sophisticated, fluid and nuanced response that displays flair and originality.

How and why does Ruth change in *Never Let Me Go*? Write about:
- how Ruth talks and behaves towards others
- how Ishiguro presents Ruth by the way he writes.   [30 marks + 4 AO4 marks]

At the start of the novel, the reader is introduced to Ruth through Kathy. This provides us with a skewed impression of her; Kathy uses the adjective phrase 'absolutely delighted' when Ruth first approaches her, suggesting that Ruth is in a position of power already (1). Kathy goes on to describe how 'Ruth led the way … very purposefully' but that 'suddenly, for no reason I could see, Ruth brought it all to an end'. The verbs 'led' and 'brought' and the adverbs 'purposefully' and 'suddenly' further emphasise Ruth's control over Kathy (2). The impression that we get of Ruth here is that she's a popular, confident girl.

Throughout Part One, Ruth is shown to manipulate those around her. She tells lies about herself, making **misleading statements** *such as 'Let's just agree. Let's agree I got it in the Sale'. Ruth often speaks in simple sentences, which creates an air of authority around what she says. The repeated use of the verb 'Let's' here shows a coercive side to her – she works very hard to present a more interesting version of herself. This is typical of young children and shows that Ruth is no different to any other child at the time (3).*

Ruth also manipulates Kathy into helping her win Tommy back (4). She does this because she is jealous of Kathy and Tommy and she does not want to leave Hailsham alone. She tells Kathy that 'Tommy and I are made for each other'. The **rhetorical** *question 'You'll do this for us, won't you, Kathy?' highlights how Ruth manipulates Kathy into feeling guilty (5). Ruth's social insecurities drive much of her action in early parts of the text; she worries about being alone and fitting in (6).*

However, Ruth is also shown to have a softer side, which reflects the realistic elements of her character. When Kathy confronts Ruth over her lies, she becomes 'upset', is 'at a complete loss of words' and is 'on the verge of tears'. The adjectives used here show a different, less confrontational side to Ruth. Soon after, she tries to make amends with Kathy by buying her a new tape. She acknowledges that 'it's not your one' but the fact that she 'tried to find it' shows a more caring, compassionate Ruth.

Ruth undergoes another change at the Cottages. Here, again fearing for her social position in the house, Ruth continues to control the relationship between herself, Kathy and Tommy (7). She is very **patronising**, *using adjectives such as 'poor little' Kathy and 'little miss' to put her down in front of the others. She does this because it is the only way she can maintain a higher position for herself in the house, as she acknowledges that the veterans are above her in the new hierarchy outside Hailsham (8).*

Again, she keeps Kathy and Tommy apart, showing that her insecurities about their relationship have not gone away. She sabotages their relationship by revealing that Kathy finds his drawings 'a hoot' and she tells Kathy that Tommy 'doesn't see you like that'. Throughout Part Two, Ishiguro shows a much more hostile, manipulative side to Ruth. Kathy describes being 'floored that Ruth would come out with *such a trick'. The **noun phrase** 'such a trick' shows Kathy's shock at the lengths Ruth would go to to get her way, and this is one of the reasons she decides to leave the Cottages.*

The turning point for Ruth is after she leaves the Cottages and starts donating (9). The reader learns that she has not had a good first donation, and that Kathy becomes her carer to support her. However, when Kathy arrives, she describes the atmosphere between the two as 'stilted and guarded'. Listing these two adjectives highlights how closed off Ruth has become. In fact, Ruth herself is presented as much more 'frail'. Her breathing comes 'less and less easily' and she is no longer as feisty.

We later learn that this awkwardness stemmed from Ruth's own regret over her past behaviour. She asks Kathy to forgive her, although she acknowledges that 'I don't really expect you to forgive me'. This simple sentence, alongside the verb 'expect', shows us that she feels personally responsible for what has happened (10). She regrets her actions, saying that she is 'not pretending [she] didn't always see' that Kathy and Tommy were better suited for each other. She acknowledges her behaviour was uncalled for with the verb 'pretending'. She 'kept [them] apart' and suggests that she has been dealing with guilt over this for quite some time.

*Ruth has had a lot of time to reflect on the past; she has matured to the point where she can admit her mistakes and make amends, not just by asking for forgiveness, but by providing Kathy and Tommy with the means to try for a deferral. She says 'What I want is for you to put it right. Put right what I messed up for you'. The use of the **pronoun** 'I' here is interesting, because while she is still being bossy and commanding, she is also recognising her own faults and taking ownership of her actions. At this point in the text, she has come to terms with her own failings. It is only after this that she can die in peace (11).*

1. The opening sentences focus on the beginning of the text and establish a clear point about Ruth. AO1
2. Relevant quotes are embedded as evidence. AO1
3. Ruth's characterisation is linked to the social context. AO3
4. The previous point is developed further. AO1
5. Analysis of structure and language is used to show what Ruth is like. AO2
6. Social context is used to link the previous point to the next point. AO1/AO3
7. Some evaluation is offered about why Ruth changes. AO1
8. Language analysis and social context are combined to show how and why Ruth changes. AO2/AO3
9. The reason for the change in Ruth's character is examined. AO1
10. A variety of language and structural analyses shows understanding of how Ishiguro conveys the reasons for Ruth's change. AO2
11. The essay ends with a quick conclusive paragraph that, like the rest of the essay, is well-written and contains some precise, sophisticated language. AO1/AO2/AO3

 ## Questions

EXAM PRACTICE

Spend 45 minutes writing an answer to the following question:

How and why does Tommy change in *Never Let Me Go*? Write about:
- how Tommy talks and behaves towards others
- how Ishiguro presents Tommy by the way he writes.

[30 marks + 4 AO4 marks]

Remember to use the plan you have already prepared.

Planning a Theme Question Response

You must be able to: understand what an exam question is asking you and prepare your response.

How might an exam question be phrased?

A typical theme question will read like this:

How does Ishiguro present issues around humanity and being human in *Never Let Me Go*? Write about:

• what some of the characters' attitudes are towards being a clone

• how Ishiguro presents some of these issues by the way he writes.

[30 marks + 4 AO4 marks]

How do I work out what to do?

The focus of the question is clear: issues about humanity and being human.

'What' and 'how' are important elements of this question.

For AO1, 'what' shows that you need to display a clear understanding of different characters' attitudes.

For AO2, 'how' makes it clear that you need to analyse the different ways in which Ishiguro's use of language, form and structure help to show these attitudes. Ideally, you should include quotations that you have learnt but, if necessary, you can make a clear reference to a specific part of the text.

You also need to remember to link your comments to the novel's context to achieve your AO3 marks and write accurately to pick up your four AO4 marks for spelling, punctuation and grammar.

How can I plan my essay?

You have approximately 45 minutes to write your essay.

This isn't long, but you should spend the first five minutes writing a quick plan. This will help you focus your response and produce a well-structured essay.

Try to come up with five to six ideas. Each of these can then be written up as a paragraph.

You can plan your response in whatever way you find most useful. Some students like to make a quick list of points, re-numbering them into a logical order. Others like to use spider diagrams; look at the example on the opposite page.

At Hailsham, the students act much like typical children. Ishiguro only slowly shows us that they are different through the things the guardians say.

However, the students are aware that they are different to 'normal' people.
'We certainly knew – though not in any deep sense – that we were different from our guardians, and also from the normal people outside.'
(Kathy: Chapter 6)
(Context: issue of cloning)

Humanity and being human

Some people, such as Madame and Miss Emily, campaign for better rights for the clones.
'I hope you can appreciate how much we *were* able to secure for you.'
(Miss Emily: Chapter 22)
(Context: human rights, ethical issues around cloning)

People from 'outside' react with fascination, disgust or pity around the students.
'But she was afraid of us in the same way someone might be afraid of spiders.'
(Kathy: Chapter 3)
(Context: ethical issues around cloning)

However, even Miss Emily admits that things will not change. People are not willing to view the clones as human because it would change their way of life.
'And though we've come a long way since then, it's still not a notion universally held, even today.'
(Miss Emily: Chapter 22)
(Context: ethical issues of cloning)

Ultimately, everyone dies, even 'normal' people. Miss Emily is shown as old and frail.
'The figure in the wheelchair was frail and contorted, and it was the voice more than anything that helped me recognise her.'
(Kathy: Chapter 21)

Summary

- Make sure you know what the focus of the essay is.
- Remember to analyse how ideas are conveyed by Ishiguro.
- Try to relate your ideas to the novel's social and historical context.

Questions

QUICK TEST
1. What key skills do you need to show in your answer?
2. What are the benefits of quickly planning your essay?
3. Why is it better to have learned quotations for the exam?

EXAM PRACTICE
Plan a response to the following exam question:

How does Ishiguro present issues around identity in *Never Let Me Go*? Write about:
- what some of the attitudes towards identity are
- how Ishiguro presents some of these issues by the way he writes.
[30 marks + 4 AO4 marks]

How does Ishiguro present issues around humanity and being human in *Never Let Me Go*? Write about:

- what some of the characters' attitudes are towards being a clone
- how Ishiguro presents some of these issues by the way he writes.

[30 marks + 4 AO4 marks]

At the start of the novel, it is not instantly clear that the students of Hailsham are different to other children. They do things that seem normal, such as make friends, have arguments with each other and struggle with puberty and relationships (1). However, Ishiguro slowly shows the reader that they are not normal through the way the guardians talk to them. For example, Miss Lucy often says that they are not told everything. When they talk about smoking, she says that it is worse for them than it is for her: 'it's much, much worse for you to smoke than it ever was for me' (2). The word 'worse' shows that there is a difference between herself and the students, suggesting that their health is more important (3).

The students know that something is different about their lives. Kathy says that they 'knew we were different'. The adjective 'different' shows that they are aware that they're not the same as everyone else. This is when we start to realise that they are clones. In the 1990s, cloning was first made possible because of Dolly the sheep, and that is when this novel is set (4). Kathy and her friends seem to be okay with that, maybe because they don't know any different (5). The guardians treat the students okay, but people outside of Hailsham don't. For example, when Madame comes she avoids them (6). When Ruth decides to test her to see if she is afraid of them, they are shocked to find out that she is. She freezes and acts like she is scared. 'She just froze and waited for us to pass by'. This metaphor shows how repulsed she was by them (7). Madame's reaction is meant to be typical of how other people would react and shows that people are afraid of the clones because they don't think they are human.

However, not everyone thinks they are totally inhuman. For example, even though Madame is afraid of the students, she still works with Miss Emily to try and get better treatment for the clones (8). We later learn that Hailsham was an experiment to prove to the rest of the world that the clones were capable of thought, creativity and even love. Miss Emily describes the 'deplorable conditions' faced by clones in other facilities, and argues that Kathy and Tommy should be thankful for the lives they got to lead (9). The adjective 'deplorable' shows that most clones live in inhuman, disgusting conditions, because most people don't feel they need more than basic living conditions (10). This is Ishiguro trying to point out the ethical issues with cloning, suggesting that some people view the clones as sub-human, while others, like Miss Emily, feel they have human qualities and deserve more.

However, at the end of the novel, Miss Emily says that things will not change; Hailsham is shut down and she says that 'things will only get worse' for clones. The verb phrase 'only get worse' shows that conditions are not improving. She says that it's too hard to stop the cloning programme, and that it's easier for people to view the clones as inhuman. Ishiguro therefore suggests that in a society where we clone people for medical advantages, we cannot view the clones as human because it would raise too many ethical issues about the entire thing (11).

1. The opening sentences establish a clear point about issues around humanity. AO1
2. A relevant quotation is used as evidence but it would be better if it was embedded in the sentence. AO1
3. Explanation of how Ishiguro conveys meaning, with some analysis of language. AO2
4. Context included. It is linked to the explanation but in a quite general way. AO3
5. The essay could be better structured as the next sentence moves on to a new point. AO1/AO4
6. The essay is clearly written but the language isn't sophisticated. AO4
7. Some detailed analysis of language features. AO2
8. Considers different sides of the issue throughout the text. AO1
9. Relevant quotation, embedded into the sentence. AO1
10. Some detailed analysis of the effects of language. AO2
11. Some detailed analysis linked to context. More subject terminology could be used. AO2/AO3

Questions

EXAM PRACTICE

Choose a paragraph of this essay. Read it through a few times, then try to rewrite and improve it. You might:

*   Improve the sophistication of the language or the clarity of expression.
*   Replace the references to the text with quotations or use better quotations.
*   Ensure quotations are embedded in the sentence.
*   Provide more detailed, or a wider range of, analysis.
*   Use more subject terminology.
*   Link some context to the analysis more effectively.

Grade 7+ Annotated Response

A proportion of the best top-band answers will be awarded Grade 8 or Grade 9. To achieve this, you should aim for a sophisticated, fluid and nuanced response that displays flair and originality.

How does Ishiguro present issues around humanity and being human in *Never Let Me Go*? Write about:

- what some of the characters' attitudes are towards being a clone
- how Ishiguro presents some of these issues by the way he writes.

[30 marks + 4 AO4 marks]

Throughout Never Let Me Go, Ishiguro deals with the subject of what it means to be human in a world where cloning is possible. Through Kathy, he presents a character who thinks and behaves in a recognisably human way, although there is always an uneasy element of her acceptance towards her purpose (1). For example, Kathy describes Hailsham as a place where 'The field was filled with playing children …' and establishes the fact that the students there struggle with friendships, and later relationships, with each other, much like a typical child would.

*However, through interjections by characters such as Miss Lucy, this seemingly normal school is shown to be unusual. Ishiguro uses Miss Lucy to make the reality of the students' lives clear to the reader. She speaks using **complex sentences**, describing how their 'lives have been set out' and that they will 'start to donate their vital organs' as they were 'created to do', highlighting the complex nature of their existence (2). Furthermore, she says that they were 'brought into this world for a purpose' and their futures 'have been decided'. The use of verbs such as 'set out', 'created', 'brought into' and 'decided' emphasise the lack of control that the students have (3). The verb 'created' is especially important, as it links clearly to the cloning process; the language used is very clinical, suggesting that clones are not born, they are made (4).*

Kathy herself acknowledges at various points that she is 'different'. When speaking about life outside of Hailsham, she describes it as 'out there' or 'the outside world'. The people themselves are described with the noun 'normals'. This establishes a clear opposition between the clones and other people, suggesting that clones are 'not normal' and are therefore less human.

They way Ishiguro portrays outsiders interacting with the students also highlights their difference from the rest of society. For example, Madame reacts with disgust; Kathy uses a metaphor comparing the students to 'spiders' to explain her reaction. Keffers is similarly described 'sighing and shaking his head disgustedly', while Ruth suggests that the woman in the art gallery would not have been so kind 'if she'd known what we really were'. Miss Emily later describes how most people viewed them as 'Shadowy objects in test tubes'. The repeated use of negative language when describing outsiders' opinions creates an atmosphere of distrust and fear towards clones (5). Sadly, this type of reaction feels realistic, as people viewed the creation of Dolly the sheep as controversial – it is likely that cloned humans would receive an even more hostile reception.

However, Ishiguro also presents a more accepting side of society through Miss Emily and Madame (6). They hoped to prove to the rest of the world that the clones 'had souls' and therefore deserved 'a more humane' existence. Miss Emily says that 'we demonstrated to the world that if students were reared in humane, cultivated environments' they could 'grow to be as sensitive and intelligent as any ordinary human being'. Interestingly, the verbs 'reared' and 'grow' again show a detached, clinical perspective of the students, suggesting that even people who disagree with their treatment do not view them as fully human. The simile 'grow to be as sensitive and intelligent as any ordinary human' further emphasises this difference. As such, Ishiguro suggests that society will never fully accept clones as human beings (7).

Ishiguro ends the novel by subtly showing the similarities between the clones and 'normals' (8). For example, both Ruth and Miss Emily are described with the adjective 'frail', suggesting that death is inevitable, regardless of your 'human' status. Even though 'normals' can live longer through the donations of the clones, they cannot escape death entirely, which makes us all the same in the end. By using Kathy as narrator, Ishiguro is able to present a sympathetic character who is both human and inhuman at the same time. The reader can recognise elements of their own life in her experiences, while also feeling some uneasiness about the differences between her upbringing and our own. The reader is left questioning what it means to be human, which is exactly what Ishiguro wanted to do; by problematising issues around cloning, he makes us question where medical science will take us in the future (9).

1. The opening sentences establish a clear point about attitudes towards humanity. AO1
2. Relevant quotes are embedded as evidence. AO2
3. Ishiguro's use of language to convey meaning is analysed in detail. AO2
4. Specific context is used to enhance the analysis. AO3
5. Detailed analysis includes a range of subject terminology. AO2
6. A new paragraph changes the focus of this well-structured essay. AO1
7. Analysis of language is enhanced by contextual links. AO2/AO3
8. The essay ends with a well-structured conclusion. There is a sense of the text as a whole, reinforced during the essay by quotations from across all three parts of the novel. AO1
9. Analysis is linked to the novel as a whole and to context. AO2/AO3

> ## Questions
>
> EXAM PRACTICE
> Spend 45 minutes writing an answer to the following question:
>
> How does Ishiguro present issues around identity in *Never Let Me Go*? Write about:
> * what some of the attitudes towards identity are
> * how Ishiguro presents some of these issues by the way he writes.
> [30 marks + 4 AO4 marks]
>
> Remember to use the plan you have already prepared.

Glossary

Abstract noun – a noun denoting an idea, quality, or state rather than a concrete object.

Adjective – a word that describes a noun.

Adverb – a word that describes a verb.

Adverbial phrase – a group of two or more words that function together as an adverb.

Analogy – a similarity or comparison between two features.

Atmosphere – the mood or emotion in a text.

Carer – a fictional role. Someone who provides emotional support to students/clones going through the donation process.

Chronological – arranged in order of time.

Clone – an organism that is genetically identical to another and from which it was derived.

Cloning – the process of producing similar populations of genetically identical individuals using DNA.

Collections – a fictional term used in the novel to describe the personal collection of second-hand goods and trinkets acquired by the students of Hailsham through the Sales and Exchanges.

Colloquial – the use of everyday language; slang.

Complete – a fictional medical term used to describe the death of a student/clone.

Complex sentence – a sentence containing one or more dependent clauses in addition to the main clause.

Compound sentence – a sentence containing two or more main clauses, linked by a conjunction.

Contemporary – present or modern times.

Connotation – when something is suggested or implied, rather than plainly stated.

Create – a verb, meaning to cause to come into being or to make. In this text, the word is used to describe how the clones come into being – they are created, not born.

Deferral – a fictional term used to describe asking for additional time before starting the donation process. The rumour states that only a couple who are truly in love can obtain a deferral.

Direct address – when the narrator addresses the audience as if they are talking to them personally.

Disguise – to conceal or cover something up.

DNA – an acronym standing for deoxyribonucleic acid: an extremely long macromolecule that is the main component of chromosomes and is the material that transfers genetic characteristics in all life forms.

Dominance – having power and influence over others.

Donor – a fictional role. Someone who is undergoing medical procedures to remove organs and/or tissue, to be given to 'normal' people.

Donate – to present as a gift.

Dramatic pause – a break, stop, or rest, often for a calculated purpose or effect.

Embryo – in mammals, the early stages of development of new life, within the womb.

Embryonic stem-cell research – stem cells derived from the undifferentiated inner mass cells of a human embryo. In research, they are used to help find ways of fighting various diseases.

Ethics (ethical) – a system of moral principles.

Fantasy/fantasise – to conceive fanciful or extravagant notions or ideas.

Fate – the idea that something is predetermined or unavoidable.

Fictional – made up or invented.

First person – a form of narration where one person speaks about themselves and their experiences.

Foreshadow – hint at future events in the text.

Gene therapy – the introduction of normal genes into cells in place of missing or defective ones to correct genetic disorders.

Guardian – a fictional role. Someone who acts in a teaching role at Hailsham.

Humane – acting in a manner that causes the least harm to people or animals.

Idealistic – to cherish or pursue a noble purpose or goals.

Imagery – words used to create a picture in the imagination.

Imperative – an order.

Longevity – the length or duration of something, often a life or service.

Manipulate – to manage or influence, often in a negative way.

Metaphor – a figure of speech in which a term or phrase is applied to something to which it is not literally applicable in order to suggest a resemblance.

Misleading statement – to give a false impression, or to be intentionally unclear, or deceptive.

Modelled – a fictional term used to describe the original people chosen for cloning.

Narrator – a person who gives an account or tells the story of events and/or experiences.

Non-linear – a plot that does not follow a chronological order.

Noun – a person, place, thing, state or quality.

Noun phrase – a group of words acting as a noun.

Passive – not reacting visibly to something that might be expected to produce an emotion or feeling.

Patronising – talking in a nice way that implies a belief in the superiority of the speaker.

Pause – a temporary stop in speech or action.

Poignant – affecting or emotional.

Possible – a fictional term for people the students/clones feel they may have been modelled on.

Pronoun – words that replace nouns and noun phrases such as I, you, he, this, who, what.

Rear – a verb, meaning to take care of and support until maturity. It can also be used to refer to breeding and raising livestock.

Recovery centre – a fictional facility where students/clones go during the donation process.

Reminisce – to recall past situations, events or experiences.

Rhetorical question – a question asked to produce an effect or to make a statement rather than to gain information.

Sales – a fictional event that took place in Hailsham. Items from charity shops were brought into the school; students could purchase items, using tokens obtained from giving their artwork to Madame or in the Exchanges.

Simile – a figure of speech in which one thing is compared with another using 'like' or 'as'.

Simple sentence – a sentence that contains only one clause.

Stem cell – a cell that upon division replaces its own numbers and gives rise to cells that differentiate further into one or more specialised types.

Sympathetic – agreement in feeling, as between persons or on the part of one person with respect to another.

Tension – a feeling of anticipation, discomfort or excitement.

Tolerance – a fair, objective and permissive attitude towards others.

Tone – the general character or attitude of a place, piece of writing, situation, etc.

Verb – a doing or action word.

Verb phrase – a group of words making up a verb.

Veterans – a fictional nickname for more experienced students/clones at the Cottages.

Answers

Quick Test
1. Tommy reacts by throwing a temper tantrum.
2. Miss Lucy tells Tommy that he doesn't have to be good at art.
3. Madame reacts by freezing on the spot; it is clear she is afraid of the students.
4. Miss Geraldine.
5. She checks the Sales registers and sees that Ruth got the pencil case there.

Exam Practice
Answers might describe how Kathy expected her friends to be honest with her. She reacts with anger when she thinks Tommy is lying: she uses the adjective 'rubbish' and tells him to stop playing 'stupid games'. In the second quote, she is shocked by Madame's reaction, despite her doing 'what we had predicted'. This verb phrase shows that she had hoped for a different outcome; she had perhaps hoped to prove Ruth wrong. For the third quote, she feels regret when she is cruel to Ruth; the prepositional phrase 'on the verge of tears' shows she immediately regrets confronting her.

Pages 6–7
Quick Test
1. Madame cries when she sees Kathy holding her pillow and dancing to 'Never Let Me Go'.
2. She reacts with anger and attempts to put them straight about their purpose in life.
3. She regrets saying that he didn't have to be good at art; instead, she encourages him to continue with his art.

Exam Practice
Answers might focus on her desire to tell the students the truth about their lives. Analysis may include the simple sentences 'Your lives are set out for you' or 'That's what each of you was created to do'. Similarly, when she tells Tommy that his 'art *is* important'; answers may focus on the use of italics to emphasise her change of heart or the noun 'evidence'.

Pages 8–9
Quick Test
1. They can come and go as they please. They are also in smaller groups and have very little adult supervision.
2. Watching television programmes.
3. Pornographic magazines.
4. Chrissie feels in awe of the people from Hailsham.
5. To see Ruth's possible.

Exam Practice
Answers might focus on Kathy's struggle to understand how to fit in or know where she comes from. Analysis might include the simple sentence 'It's not something worth copying', which shows that she doesn't think mimicking actors on television is appropriate, or the compound sentences 'I hardly saw the contorted bodies, because I was focusing on the faces' or the verb phrase 'I checked each model's face before moving on', which suggests that her fascination with the pornographic magazines was more about finding her possible and explaining her own sexual urges.

Pages 10–11
Quick Test
1. She reacts with anger, emphasising her disappointment.
2. They find Kathy's lost 'Never Let Me Go' tape.
3. He thinks that the artwork is used to prove that students are really in love and therefore deserve a deferral.
4. Ruth tells Kathy that Tommy doesn't like her in a romantic way.

Exam Practice
Answers might focus on Ruth's negative, angry or manipulative side. Analysis might include the tone of voice Ruth uses when she says 'We're modelled from *trash*'. The use of italics here highlights her anger. She goes on to list the type of people she thinks they are modelled on, highlighting her disappointment. In the third quote, analysis could include the patronising tone she uses when saying 'Well, Kathy, what you have to realise is that Tommy doesn't see you like that'. This shows a darker, more manipulative side to her character.

Pages 12–13
Quick Test
1. Hailsham was closed.
2. To see the abandoned boat.
3. Ruth admits that she kept them apart.
4. She wants Kathy and Tommy to try and get a deferral – she wants to make up for her past mistakes.
5. Ruth told Kathy she thought she should become Tommy's carer; just before Ruth completes, Kathy agrees to do it.

Exam Practice
For the first quote, answers may focus on the slow realisation that Ruth was no longer as strong as she once was. Analysis could include the verb phrase 'it was then ... that Tommy seemed to become aware for the first time' as well as the adjective 'frail' used to describe Ruth. With the second quote, answers may focus on how it took so long for Ruth to admit to keeping Tommy and Kathy apart. The fact that she speaks in such a short complex sentence seems almost anti-climactic, after such a long build-up. In the third quote, answers may focus on Kathy's use of a complex sentence, exploring all the reasons why her relationship with Tommy was so tragic. She lists the adjectives 'ridiculous, reprehensible' to describe their delayed attempts at staying together.

Pages 14–15
Quick Test
1. The deferrals are just a rumour; they are not real.
2. Miss Lucy was fired because she wanted to tell the students the truth about their existence.
3. After his fourth donation.

Exam Practice
Answers might focus on Miss Emily's blunt honesty or her idealistic views of Hailsham. Analysis might include the verbs 'reveal', 'prove', 'kept', '*fooled*', 'sheltered' and 'gave', which she uses to justify her decision to keep things from the students. The use of italics with the word 'fooled' is the closest she comes to admitting that her actions were negative. Similarly, her use of simple sentences when telling Tommy about deferrals or her dismissive tone when justifying her actions further support her lack of regret over the past.

Pages 16–17
Quick Test
1. She is a conversational, first-person narrator.
2. Hailsham, the Cottages and the recovery centres.
3. Kathy's memories are not in chronological order.

Exam Practice
Answers may focus on Kathy's unreliability, her obsession with the past, the non-linear way she talks or how she foreshadows things to come. In quote one, analysis may include her use of compound sentences to justify her inability to let go of the past; they suggest that she has tried to move on, but that she does not want to. In the second quote, analysis could include

the prepositional phrase 'a long time ago', which suggests that she may not remember accurately. Quote three shows how Kathy uses direct address to talk to the reader.

Pages 18–19
Quick Test
1. To show that there was a more humane way to rear clones, providing them with an education and information on how to survive independently.
2. A collection of farm houses.
3. Clones donate their body parts one at a time until they die.

Exam Practice
Answers may focus on the sheltered experience of Hailsham, the more barren and isolated experiences at the Cottages or the differences between recovery centres. In quote one, analysis may include the adjectives 'long narrow' used to describe Hailsham. For the second quote, analysis could include the way Kathy lists the various structures of the farm, with the verb 'converted', which suggests it was changed from accommodating animals to humans. Finally, analysis of the third quote could include a comparison of how Kingsfield 'falls way short' of Ruth's centre, which is described using the adjectives 'gleaming' tiles and 'double-glazed windows'.

Pages 20–21
Quick Test
1. Ishiguro himself attended a grammar school, which may have influenced his descriptions of Hailsham. His parents also sheltered him from their experiences in Japan during World War II, which is similar to how Miss Emily sheltered the students from the outside world. He also studied philosophy, which is the study of concepts such as existence and knowledge, which feature in the text.
2. Miss Emily describes a world that remains uncomfortable with the ethics of cloning; human cloning is currently illegal for this reason. Answers may also focus on the Morningdale scandal – in our society, there is opposition to interference or research surrounding human embryos.
3. Ishiguro touches on philosophical issues such as what it means to be human, morality, right and wrong, freedom, information and knowledge, reason, creativity and justice.

Exam Practice
Comments might include Miss Emily's tone when she says ' … well by then it was too late' alongside the use of ellipsis to show her defeatist attitude, which links to those who argue for the progress of medical science. When she says 'Yes, there *were* arguments', the use of italics for '*were*' suggest anger and resentment, linking to ethical debates around cloning.

Pages 22–23
Quick Test
1. Providing clones with access to the internet or television would allow them unrestricted access to knowledge from the outside world. It could have a negative impact on their physical and mental well-being. Alternatively, they could use technology to resist their fate and rebel.
2. Because they have no other basis for reference regarding how to act in the outside world.
3. Without technology, the clones have limited knowledge of the wider world. They are reliant on knowledge obtained from those around them, which is a very small, isolated community of people (such as the guardians, caretakers such as Keffers, other clones, nurses and doctors).

Exam Practice
Comments may include Kathy's reference to listening to 'tapes', or how the music Judy Bridgewater produced was 'not the sort of thing any of us at Hailsham liked'. Kathy uses the adjectives 'cocktail-bar stuff', which would not have appealed to many teens at the time. However, contextually, many teenagers in the 1990s would have had their own Walkman, so when Kathy uses the prepositional phrase 'a few years before' they started appearing in the Sales, the reader realises her access to technology would have been second-hand.

Pages 24–25
Quick Test
1. Kathy has been a carer for longer because she is good at it. She gets to choose some of her donors.
2. Kathy has fond memories of her time at Hailsham.
3. Kathy is accepting of her fate.

Exam Practice
Answers may focus on Kathy's pride in her role as carer or her strong connection to the past. Analysis in the first quote could focus on her use of the adjectives 'much better' or 'impressive' to describe her work as a carer. She uses italics, as well as the interjection 'Okay' when she says 'Okay, maybe I *am* boasting now' to show how proud she is of her work as a carer. In the second quote, analysis could focus on Kathy's angry tone of voice when she realises that 'Ruth kept pretending to forget things about Hailsham'. The adverbial phrase 'I got more and more irritated with her' further emphasises how strongly Kathy feels about Hailsham; she doesn't like it when Ruth tries to move on. Analysis of the third quote could include the repetition of the verb 'lost', which emphasises that while Kathy knows that she will 'lose' the physical presences of Ruth and Tommy, her memories will remain. The adverbial phrase 'I don't see them ever fading' further highlights this.

Pages 26–27
Quick Test
1. Ruth manipulates others by excluding them from her social circle, telling lies, using guilt, asking people to do things for her or turning people's words against them.
2. She is jealous of Kathy and Tommy's relationship.
3. Ruth hopes for a future where deferrals are real and where she could work in an office.

Exam Practice
Analysis of the first quote might include Ruth's use of rhetorical questions and her guilt when getting Kathy involved in her relationship with Tommy. She uses the personal pronoun 'you' to flatter Kathy and to convince her to become involved. In the second quote, her patronising tone and the adjective 'sweety' are manipulative. She speaks in simple sentences, which highlight her anger and aggression. In the third quote, Ruth's repeated use of the personal pronoun 'I' shows that she takes ownership of her past actions. Her use of simple sentences show openness and honesty.

Pages 28–29
Quick Test
1. He rises to the bullying; the students find this funny.
2. He is afraid that it will affect future opportunities for him, such as deferrals.
3. Tommy becomes more mature and his rages occur less frequently. He questions everything around him and is perceptive and critical of what is happening. He does not want Kathy to see him weak, whereas in the past he often showed her his weaker side.

Exam Practice
Analysis may focus on how he starts out quite immature, but that through his conversations with Miss Lucy and Kathy he begins to change. For example, in the first quote he shows maturity by being able to admit to changing. He uses a simple sentence to show how the conversation with Miss Lucy helped him to calm down. Answers for the second quote may focus on how the reader feels sympathy for Tommy in Part Two of the novel. Analysis may include Ruth's dismissive tone when using the noun phrase 'he isn't like a real Hailsham student'. In the third quote, Tommy is presented as shocked. He asks Miss Emily a lot of questions to clarify his understanding. Analysis may include the questions 'It was all about what you told us? It was nothing more than that?', which show how dejected he is to learn that deferrals are not real.

Answers

Pages 30–31

Quick Test

1. At first, Miss Lucy tells Tommy he does not need to be artistic. However, she later changes her mind and tells him that his artwork is important evidence for later in life, and suggests that he has not been told enough about his future.
2. She tells him to continue making artwork for his own sake, and because it is valuable evidence.
3. She was fired because she wanted to tell the students more about their lives.

Exam Practice

Comments might focus on the verbs 'shaking' and the repeated use of the adjective 'furious' when describing her actions. This shows that she is very angry at the way the students are taught. She also repeats the verb phrase 'You've been told and not told' often. Her use of simple sentences, such as when she says 'But I'm not' highlights her anger, again directed at how the students have been taught about their futures. In the third quote, she uses the pronoun 'they' to distance herself from the leadership at Hailsham. She feels that the students should be told more, but she does not want to be the one to tell them.

Pages 32–33

Quick Test

1. Hailsham was created to show the world that clones were capable of thought and creativity, and were therefore deserving of more humane treatment.
2. She is proud of what they accomplished. In her mind, she has protected the students from the horrible conditions faced by other clones.
3. She feels pride in them, but thinks they should be grateful for what she achieved for them. She pities them.

Exam Practice

Analysis could focus on the abstract noun 'disappointments', comparing this to the adverbial phrase 'I don't feel so badly about it', or the way she speaks using the pronoun 'we', which takes some of the pressure away from her own failings. The verbs 'protected' and 'absorbed' show her pride in providing a more humane upbringing.

Pages 34–35

Quick Test

1. To show people in the outside world that the students at Hailsham have souls and are deserving of more humane treatment.
2. She admits to being afraid of them, but she feels sorry for them too.
3. She regrets what happened at Hailsham, and wishes she could have accomplished more for the clones.

Exam Practice

Answers might focus on how our initial impression of Madame is that she is rigid and afraid of the students. This changes later, as the reader sees a passionate, sympathetic character.

Analysis might focus on the verbs 'shudder' from Kathy's initial impression of Madame. This can be compared to later, when Madame asks the students a lot of simple questions, such as 'You believe this? That you're deeply in love?' and 'Why should they be grateful?' or 'What did we do to you?'. Similarly, her use of the metaphor 'poor creatures' shows that she is both sympathetic and angry.

Pages 36–37

Quick Test

1. Keffers is a caretaker/handyman. He fixes things around the farm and brings food and fuel.
2. Ruth looks up to Chrissie and Rodney because they are older and have been at the Cottages longer.
3. Chrissie is in awe of the students from Hailsham. She thinks they have had a special upbringing.

Exam Practice

Answers might focus on how other clones view Hailsham as a special place, one that gives alumni different rights and experiences. Analysis might focus on the 'mysterious' tone Ruth would 'encourage' about being from Hailsham, the view that there was a 'separate set of rules' for Hailsham students and Chrissie's use of the adjective 'lucky' to describe Hailsham students.

Pages 38–39

Quick Test

1. Kathy confronts Ruth about her pencil case, implying that she knows Ruth has been lying.
2. Ruth tells Tommy that Kathy thinks his drawings are humorous.
3. She asks forgiveness for lying to Kathy about her urges and for keeping Kathy and Tommy apart.

Exam Practice

Answers may focus on the tumultuous relationship between Ruth and Kathy, or on the overall positive influence Kathy feels Ruth had on her life. Analysis may consider the adverbial phrase 'utterly baffling' or the adjective 'dearest' to emphasise Kathy's confusion towards humiliating Ruth in Chapter 5.

Analysis of the second quote could include the verb 'floored' and the abstract noun 'trick', which show Kathy's disappointment at Ruth's betrayal of her trust in Chapter 16. Finally, analysis of the use of the adjective 'grateful' shows Kathy's true feelings about her relationship with Ruth; despite their ups and downs, she always treasured their friendship.

Pages 40–41

Quick Test

1. She begins to realise she has feelings for Tommy.
2. It shows the reader that Tommy has feelings for Kathy.
3. Ishiguro suggests that Tommy doesn't want her to see him in pain/suffering.

Exam Practice

Answers may focus on their close relationship throughout the text and the fact that they confide in each other. Analysis of the first quote may consider the prepositional phrase 'drift towards him' or the verb phrase 'I kept going', which shows Kathy's early concern for Tommy was unexpected. Analysis of the second quote could include the adverb 'together' combined with the verb phrase 'finding ourselves side by side again' to show their increasing closeness in Part Two. Finally, analysis of the third quote could include Tommy's metaphor about the 'two people … in the water', which represents his relationship with Kathy, suggesting that they are holding on to something that won't last.

Pages 42–43

Quick Test

1. Through their artwork and the items in their collections.
2. Being creative, through art, writing or music, is something they can use to accumulate items in the Sales or at the Exchanges. Creative property becomes a sort of currency among the students.
3. Possibles would give the students some idea about where they came from.
4. People in the outside world view the students with disgust and fear. They do not want to view them as anything other than a medical supply.
5. Miss Emily and Madame feel that the students are deserving of better treatment. They feel they should live happy, full lives, even if their time is brief.

Exam Practice

Answers may focus on the students' desire to explore how outsiders view them or their acceptance of being different. Analysis of the first quote may focus on the adverbial phrase used to suggest that the students' self-worth was tied closely to their ability to be creative. In the second quote, analysis may include Ruth's use of the question 'Do you think she'd have talked to us like that if she'd known what we really were?', which suggests the woman in the art gallery would have been disgusted had she known they were clones; Ruth says this as though it is an insult. It suggests that they should be ashamed of themselves. The tone Kathy uses to describe Miss Emily's reaction is very matter-of-fact; she questions 'why would anyone doubt you had a soul?', which shows she supports the idea that clones do have souls. The fronted adverbial 'As you say' shows that the clones themselves believe this.

Pages 44–45

Quick Test

1. She spends a lot of time on her own, driving from one donor to another. Once Ruth and Tommy have completed, Kathy has lost all ties to her past; her memories are all she has left.
2. Hailsham was different, more humane, than most clone facilities. The impression of other facilities is very poor; talking about Hailsham provided them with comforting thoughts.
3. She gets angry when other people forget things. This is because she places so much value on her memories; when others forget things that are important to her, it devalues her own beliefs.

Exam Practice

Answers may focus on the happy memories Kathy has of her past, particularly Hailsham, in contrast to other clones, who would rather forget their experiences. For the first quote, comments might include the nouns 'blotches' and 'grimace', paired with the adverb 'desperately', which suggests that he had bad experiences in the past, ones that he'd rather forget. In the second quote, the adverb 'still' suggests that, despite so much time passing, Kathy looks back on her past with fond memories and hopes to find the school again. Analysis of the third quote could include the complex sentence in which she lists the things she's lost. The contrasting parts of the sentence suggest that while they're physical presence is gone, her memories of them will always remain.

Pages 46–47

1. They go through ups and downs, fight, argue, play games, fantasise and gossip.
2. Their relationship is realistic because it has the 'ups and downs' that many people experience in their own friendships. They sometimes argue and disagree, but ultimately they remain lifelong friends.
3. Ruth wants Tommy and Kathy to go for a deferral; she thinks they have a real chance of getting one and wants to make up for keeping them apart in the past.

Exam Practice

Answers might focus on the relationship between Ruth and Kathy. Analysis of the first quote may include the noun phrase 'no doubt she was the leader', which shows how Kathy was accepting of Ruth's control whilst at Hailsham. In the second quote, the verbs 'squeezed' and 'thanked' show a more tender moment between Kathy and Ruth. Analysis of the third quote could include the abstract noun 'precious possessions', showing how much Kathy valued her only lasting gift from Ruth. Kathy's tone, when talking about Ruth, is often reverential.

Pages 48–49

Quick Test

1. Because she is jealous.
2. They think being in love will get a deferral.
3. She questions how the students know they're truly in love.

Exam Practice

Answers may consider how Ishiguro subtly establishes a relationship between Kathy and Tommy throughout the text. Analysis may include the prepositional phrase 'been friends with Tommy for years'. The tone in which Kathy and Tommy speak to each other is also notable for its comfortable, easy nature. There are undertones of regret and sadness when they do end up together because their time together as a couple is brief.

Pages 50–51

Quick Test

1. She thinks it is cruel for them to dream of a future they won't have.
2. She wanted to find out about where she came from; the fact that the woman worked in an office, which was Ruth's dream, would have explained her desire for this type of life.
3. She thinks it provides the students with hope.
4. Because they were privileged; they got to live a more humane, ordinary life.

Exam Practice

Answers may focus on the students' desires to live full lives, comparing this to differing views among the guardians. Analysis could include Miss Lucy's repetition of the pronoun 'none of you', in which she effectively stops the students from making plans; she felt that this was unfair, considering that their lives were already chosen for them. This can be compared with Miss Emily's use of the abstract nouns 'dream' and 'fantasy' alongside the question 'What harm is there?'. Unlike Miss Lucy, Miss Emily felt that allowing the students to make plans for their future was not a negative thing. Ruth's positive optimism is evident when she urges Kathy and Tommy to 'try and get a deferral'. She uses the simple sentence 'A real chance' to show how hopeful she is for them.

Pages 52–53

Quick Test

1. The fences at Hailsham are not electrified.
2. Sign out in Keffers's ledgerbook.
3. She drives from one recovery centre to another in her role as carer.

Exam Practice

Answers may focus on the lack of freedom afforded to the students, the control exerted over them even when they leave Hailsham and their desire for some personal freedom and choice. Analysis may include the adjective 'terrible', which suggests that at other rearing facilities clones are killed trying to escape. The verb 'wandered' suggests that there is more freedom at the Cottages for the students to travel. Finally, the pronouns 'my' and the verb 'have' show how, as the clones get older, they gain more personal freedom to travel the country and spend time on their own.

Pages 54–55

Quick Test

1. They experience everyday issues such as bullying, trying to fit in, new relationships, moving school/house and self-acceptance.
2. To donate body parts to the 'normal' people in society.
3. To prove that the clones were capable of abstract thought – to obtain better treatment for the clones.
4. People had become too reliant on the benefits provided by the clones; they did not want to change this beneficial situation.

Exam Practice

Answers may focus on how the students, or clones, were viewed as sub-human. Analysis may focus on Miss Lucy's contrasting use of the pronouns 'you' and 'me', which establish clear differences between the importance of health

Answers

for the guardians and for the students. The prepositional phrase 'out there' and the adjective 'different' further emphasise the differences between the clones and 'normal' people; the students view the outside world itself as separate from Hailsham. Finally, the italics used in verb phrase '*to prove you had souls at all*' emphasises the different views that people held about the clones.

Pages 56–57
Quick Test
1. To protect them from the truth about who they are and to ensure that they participate in their studies.
2. She wants to tell the students the truth about their lives.
3. Ruth lies about the following: chess; Miss Geraldine and her pencil case; Tommy's feelings for Kathy; Kathy's 'urges'; the privileges afforded from being a Hailsham student.
4. She doesn't admit her feelings for Tommy until it is too late, nor does she acknowledge the reason behind her fascination with pornography.

Exam Practice
Answers might focus on how the guardians, and Miss Emily, lie to the students about their futures, how the students lie to each other as part of growing up and maturing or how they lie to themselves. Analysis could include the prepositional phrase 'a long time ago' because it shows that even the narrator may get things wrong as she is looking back on things that happened in the past. The adverb 'explicitly' suggests that Ruth doesn't lie outright to others, but does so subtly through her actions. The verb phrase 'know who you are' also suggests that the guardians have kept important information from the students, including their ultimate purpose in life.

Pages 62–63
Quick Test
1. Understanding the whole text, specific analysis and terminology, awareness of the relevance of context, a well-structured essay and accurate writing.
2. Planning focuses your thoughts and allows you to produce a well-structured essay.
3. Quotations give you more opportunities to do specific AO2 analysis.

Exam Practice
Answers might focus on how Tommy is quite immature and impulsive in Part One. In Part Two he begins to take responsibility for himself more. In Part Three, Tommy has matured and is more hopeful and accepting; at the very end, he accepts his fate, and wishes to face it alone.

Pages 66–67 and 72–73
Use the mark scheme provided below to self-assess your strengths and weaknesses. Work up from the bottom, putting a tick by things you have fully accomplished, a ½ by skills that are in place but need securing and underlining areas that need development. The grade boundaries are included so you can assess your progress towards your target grade.

Pages 68–69
Quick Test
1. Understanding the whole text, specific analysis and terminology, awareness of the relevance of context, a well-structured essay and accurate writing.
2. Planning focuses your thoughts and allows you to produce a well-structured essay.
3. Quotations give you more opportunities to do specific AO2 analysis.

Exam Practice
Ideas might include the following: creating and trading creative goods at Exchanges; collecting personal items for their collections at the Sales; having their work selected by Madame for her Gallery; Kathy's acceptance that she was 'different'; their goals for the future; the students' fascination with their possibles; Kathy's search for faces in pornographic magazines; Ruth's anger in Cromer; gauging the reaction of 'normal people'; or even being from Hailsham itself.

Grade	AO1 (12 marks)	AO2 (12 marks)	AO3 (6 marks)	AO4 (4 marks)
6–7+	A convincing, well-structured essay that answers the question fully. Quotations and references are well-chosen and integrated into sentences.	Analysis of the full range of Ishiguro's methods. Thorough exploration of the effects of these methods. Accurate range of subject terminology.	Exploration is linked to specific aspects of the novel's contexts to show detailed understanding.	Consistent high level of accuracy. Vocabulary and sentences are used to make ideas clear and precise.
4–5	A clear essay that always focuses on the exam question. Quotations and references support ideas effectively. The response refers to different points in the novel.	Explanations of Ishiguro's different methods. Clear understanding of the effects of these methods. Accurate use of subject terminology.	References to relevant aspects of context to show clear understanding.	Good level of accuracy. Vocabulary and sentences help to keep ideas clear.
2–3	The essay has some good ideas that are mostly relevant. Some quotations and references are used to support ideas.	Identification of some different methods used by Ishiguro to convey meaning. Some subject terminology.	Some awareness of how ideas in the novel link to its context.	Reasonable level of accuracy. Errors do not get in the way of the essay making sense.